T'ang Pottery and Porcelain

THE FABER MONOGRAPHS ON POTTERY AND PORCELAIN

Present Editors: R. J. CHARLESTON *and* MARGARET MEDLEY
Former Editors: W. B. HONEY, ARTHUR LANE *and* SIR HARRY GARNER

WORCESTER PORCELAIN AND LUND'S BRISTOL *by* Franklin A. Barrett

DERBY PORCELAIN
by Franklin A. Barrett *and* Arthur L. Thorpe

APOTHECARY JARS *by* Rudolf E. A. Drey

ENGLISH DELFTWARE *by* F. H. Garner *and* Michael Archer

ORIENTAL BLUE AND WHITE *by* Sir Harry Garner

CHINESE CELADON WARES
by G. St. G. M. Gompertz

MASON PORCELAIN AND IRONSTONE
by Reginald Haggar *and* Elizabeth Adams

NEW HALL AND ITS IMITATORS *by* David Holgate

LATER CHINESE PORCELAIN *by* Soame Jenyns

JAPANESE POTTERY *by* Soame Jenyns

JAPANESE PORCELAIN *by* Soame Jenyns

FRENCH FAÏENCE *by* Arthur Lane

GREEK POTTERY *by* Arthur Lane

YÜAN PORCELAIN AND STONEWARE *by* Margaret Medley

T'ANG POTTERY AND PORCELAIN *by* Margaret Medley

MEDIEVAL ENGLISH POTTERY *by* Bernard Rackham

CREAMWARE *by* Donald C. Towner

ENGLISH BLUE AND WHITE PORCELAIN OF THE EIGHTEENTH
CENTURY
by Bernard Watney

LONGTON HALL PORCELAIN *by* Bernard Watney

T'ANG
POTTERY AND
PORCELAIN

by
MARGARET MEDLEY

FABER AND FABER
London · Boston

First published in 1981
by Faber and Faber Limited
3 Queen Square London WC1
Filmset and printed in Great Britain by
BAS Printers Limited
Over Wallop, Hampshire
All rights reserved

other books by the author

YÜAN PORCELAIN AND STONEWARE
THE CHINESE POTTER: A PRACTICAL HISTORY OF CHINESE CERAMICS
KOREAN AND CHINESE CERAMICS
CHINESE PAINTING AND THE DECORATIVE STYLE
HANDBOOK OF CHINESE ART

British Library Cataloguing in Publication Data

Medley, Margaret
T'ang pottery and porcelain
(Faber monograph on pottery and porcelain)
1. Pottery, Chinese – T'ang-Five dynasties, 618–906
2. Porcelain, Chinese – T'ang-Five dynasties, 618–906
I. Title
738'.0951   NK4165.3
ISBN 0-571-10957-8

PREFACE

When the late Sir Harry Garner suggested the possibility of writing about T'ang pots and putting them into some kind of perspective, I welcomed the opportunity. The period is full of interest and there is, artistically, much of the excitement that is also characteristic of the Yüan period. It was an age of expansion and of rapid cultural change following revitalizing contacts with foreign peoples. Had I known as much then as I have now learned, it seems likely that I might have been less enthusiastic, for of all periods it is probably the most difficult, because most lacking in dated material. So much of what we have has come from rifled rather than scientifically excavated tombs and sites, that a chronology is virtually impossible to propose. Nevertheless, something had to be attempted. It has to be admitted, then, that my book must be regarded as to some extent hypothetical, if not speculative, since I have been guided in the stonewares by the technical aspects of ceramic development, and in the figures by the changing fashions of women in looks, hair-style and clothing, flimsy enough hooks on which to hang a chronology, but the best that seemed available.

The writing of these chapters has brought home to me the fact that the book is in some measure premature. This is especially likely to prove the case with regard to Yüeh and the south China kilns of which we are still amazingly ignorant. Even so, I believe that much that is useful will be found in the following pages. In them I owe a particular debt of gratitude to Mary Tregear for her advice on the chapter on Yüeh, and my thanks are due to many friends and colleagues for their help at every stage. I must especially thank Miss Pauline Fortune for her tireless typing and retyping of a most difficult manuscript.

London, May 1979   MARGARET MEDLEY

CONTENTS

ILLUSTRATIONS

COLOUR PLATES

MAP

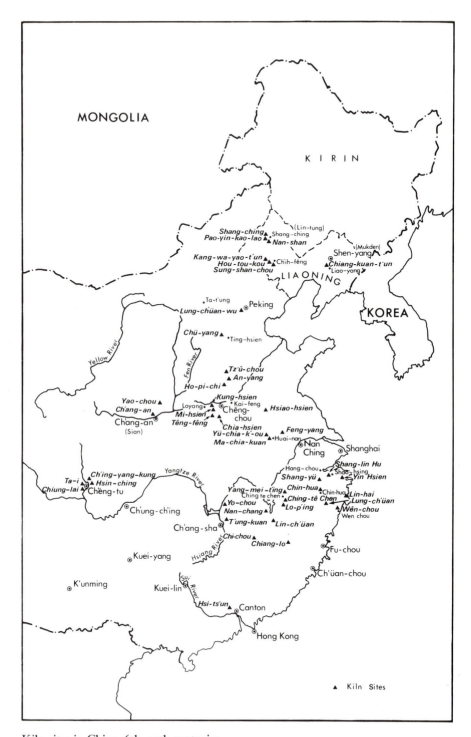

MONGOLIA

K I R I N

(Lin-tung)
Shang-ching▲ Shang-ching
Pao-yin-kao-lao▲ ▲*Nan-shan*

Kang-wa-yao-t'un▲ (Mukden)
Hou-tou-kou▲ ▲·Chih-fêng ·Shen-yang
Sung-shan-chou LIAONING ▲*Chiang-kuan-t'un*
·Liao-yang

·Ta-t'ung
Lung-chüan-wu▲ ◎Peking KOREA

Chü-yang▲ ·Ting-hsien

Yellow River ▲*Tz'ŭ-chou*
Fen River ▲*An-yang*
Ho-pi-chi▲

Yao-chou▲ *Kung-hsien*▲
Ch'ang-an▲ Loyang· ·Kai-fêng ▲*Hsiao-hsien*
Chang-an◎ *Mi-hsien*▲ ◎*Chêng-*
(Sian) *Têng-fêng*▲ *chou*
Chia-hsien▲ ▲*Feng-yang*
Yü-chia-k'-ou▲ ·Huai-nan
Ma-chia-kuan▲ ◎*Nan*
Ching
◎Shanghai
Ch'ing-yang-kung Yangtze River Hang-chou· ▲*Shang-lin Hu*
Ta-i▲ *Hsin-ching*▲ *Shang-yü*▲ ▲Shao-hsing *Yin Hsien*
Chiung-lai▲ Chêng-tu ▲*Chin-hua* Chin-hua·▲ *Lin-hai*
Yang-mei-t'ing▲ ▲*Ching-tê Chen* ▲*Lung-ch'üan*
◎Ch'ung-ch'ing Ching te chen· ▲*Lo-p'ing* ▲*Wên-chou*
Yo-chou▲ Wen chou
Nan-chang▲
◎Ch'ang-sha *T'ung-kuan*▲ ▲*Lin-ch'üan*
Chi-chou▲
Hsiang River *Chiang-lo*▲ ◎Fu-chou
◎Kuei-yang
◎Ch'üan-chou
◎K'unming Kuei-lin Sui River
Hsi-ts'un▲ ◎Canton

◎Hong Kong

▲ Kiln Sites

Kiln sites in China, 6th–10th centuries

Chapter 1
INTRODUCTION

The very name T'ang dynasty conjures up a vision of wealth, sophistication, and splendour of a kind that no other Chinese dynastic name can evoke. There springs to the mind's eye a picture of richly caparisoned horses, gay clothes, dancers, musicians, merchants of all nations, vast teeming cities into which the wealth of Asia seems to pour in a steady stream. There comes to mind a sense of a robust forward-looking people of education, endowed with a keen appreciation of the arts. And indeed there was a delight in the arts, but there was also a craving for the novel and the exotic, especially in the earlier part of the period. All this certainly contributed to a rich and colourful age. Perhaps the fact that in later centuries, especially during the Ming dynasty, the period was referred to as 'glorious T'ang' in part colours our attitude, even more than the fact that it brings to an end a prolonged period of internal conflict from which relatively little, apart from the great Buddhist sculptures, survives. In ceramics we would be at fault if we thought that what was achieved in the three hundred years of T'ang was entirely unheralded. Much was being accomplished in the preceding century and a half, although improvements were slow and very gradual. Developments in all areas, in the seventh and eighth centuries especially, could not have occurred without the reunification under the short-lived Sui dynasty, when quite suddenly the changes began to be speeded up as new influences came into play.

The reunification of China, achieved between 580 and 589, marks the opening of a new era. North China had suffered far more than the south during the centuries since the fall of Han in A.D. 220, but that area had to some extent always been open to the West and the trade from Transoxiana, so that wars were matched by cultural interchange.[1] Under Sui and later under T'ang the benefits of the contact with western Central Asia were to be reaped. In effect Sui set the stage for the great drama to be played out by T'ang.[2]

1. The history of relations between the northern Chinese dynasties, especially Northern and Western Wei and Northern Ch'i, and the cities and states of the western regions is extremely complex. Until relatively recently little work has been done in this area. What is available for reference is chiefly in journals, some of which are not easy of access. W. Barthold's *Turkestan Down to the Mongol Invasion*, London, 1928, provides even now a useful starting point.
2. Woodbridge Bingham, *The Founding of the T'ang Dynasty*, 1941, is still a valuable study, and I have drawn on it in the following paragraphs.

In setting the stage for T'ang the most culturally valuable contribution made by Sui (589–618) in the preparation for the new achievements, was the foreign policy adopted in relation to the Central Asian problem presented by the Turks. Ironically they hastened their own downfall and prepared the way for the T'ang conquests in Central Asia by military action combined with diplomatic intrigue.[3] In the last twenty years of their power the Sui kept open the trade routes, which were in fact essential to the survival of the semi-nomadic tribes of the north-west. By the time the T'ang came to power the Turks, already weakened by internal dissension, were in no position to withstand the Chinese advance into Central Asia as far as the T'ien-shan and the independent oasis states of the far side of the Tarim Basin.

During the opening years of Sui under the Emperor Wên there had been great improvements made in the internal communications system, canals being built and roads extended, both of which contributed to the potential prosperity of the empire. Unfortunately this prosperity was not attained, owing mainly to the appalling extravagance of the second emperor, Yang. Although the Emperor Yang's opening years were full of promise he failed either to add to or even to sustain the achievements of his father. Unrest became apparent within a few years of his ascent to the throne in 605, and by 613 rebellions had begun to break out. Then in 618 the Li family, of partly Central Asian origin, as well as being related to the Sui emperor, came in from the north of China and took over as the new dynasty house, the T'ang. The first emperor with the help of his son and successor, the Emperor T'ai-tsung, succeeded in establishing the family firmly as the new ruling house, building on the foundations laid by Sui. T'ang brought in efficient administration and pursued a vigorous foreign policy which resulted in a vast westward expansion. Nothing could have been more beneficial at this point to the economic, social and cultural climate. With internal peace following quickly on the period of rebellion, and with the influx of new ideas from the west, people could look forward to an era of considerable prosperity.

The great period of stability and wealth of T'ang continued from the second quarter of the seventh century until about the middle of the eighth and was mainly due to an efficient central administration, good internal com-munications based on the Sui achievement and a lively trans-Asiatic trade. Thus tax-exempt members of society such as the officials and members of the nobility built up land holdings, always regarded as marks of privilege, but which later were to prove indirectly an element contributing to disaster. Buddhist monasteries, which were also exempt from tax, accumulated huge wealth in land, and real wealth made it possible for them to employ their capital in financing industry and trade, while the merchants, who were without lands as well as being largely untaxed, were able to make great profits and create an

---

3. W. Samolin, *Eastern Turkestan to the Twelfth Century*, The Hague, 1964, and Bingham, op. cit., pp. 25–36 and 46–50.

efficient system of credit finance.[4] During this period China enjoyed unrivalled international prestige and Ch'ang-an became the cultural centre of Asia. A large foreign population brought new colour and customs to China, and the merchants profited from the trade in novelties.

Then in 756 came the An Lu-shan rebellion, which rent the Chinese state. The two capitals, Ch'ang-an and Loyang were occupied by the rebels, Ch'ang-an being sacked by them, and again to be sacked in 763 by the Tibetans. The great rebellion and the Tibetan invasion which quickly followed, dealt the Empire a blow from which it could not wholly recover. Some degree of stability was won back at about the beginning of the ninth century, but it did not last and the ninth century saw a steady decline, as the central government lost power to the military governors in the provinces, especially to those in the north-east, who ceased to pay any taxes, retaining the local revenues for their own administrations.

The development of pottery in this long period shares much of the splendour of the early years of the Empire. The potters inherited well-established traditions in stonewares, while white wares of a porcellanous nature were still in an early stage of their development into true porcelain later in the dynasty. The lead-glazed wares, perhaps largely on account of the bright colouring which is natural to them, enjoyed huge popularity, albeit it mainly as tomb furniture.

The potters themselves show a readiness to accept new ideas, meet new challenges, and supply wares that often responded to novel demands. It was during the T'ang dynasty that for the first time kilns became associated with particular wares. The association may be noticed in the contemporary literature: for example Yüeh is specifically referred to for the first time, so too is the 'yellow ware of Shou-chou'. In both these cases kiln sites have been located and excavated, those of Yüeh in the vicinity of Shang-lin Hu having first been located in 1929, and those near Shou-chou as recently as 1960. The wares of Hsing-chou however continue to be a problem, and one not now likely to be solved. No kilns have been found in the traditionally accepted location and it seems improbable that they ever will be. If they existed at all they will be buried very deeply below the surface of the north China plain, as a result of centuries of repeated flooding by the Yellow River, quite apart from the occasional changes of course of that great waterway.

It is the continuing search for the pure white body, such as that associated with the name of Hsing, that is of the greatest importance in the history of ceramics. The successful achievement of a pure white ware is of uncertain date as is also the first manufacture of a pure white porcelain. But no sooner had these white wares appeared than they became popular not only in China but also overseas from Indonesia to Egypt.

The fundamental change in T'ang was that from earthenware to stoneware,

4. D. C. Twitchett, *The Financial Administration of the T'ang Dynasty*, Cambridge, 1963, pp. 28, 31 and 72.

and earthenwares, although continuing to be made in some places, gradually faded from the scene in the course of the second half of the dynasty, surviving for vessels in the north-east and in the Liao tradition in Manchuria, and persisting to modern times in glazed tiles.

The shapes of the pottery, especially of the first half of the period, reflect strongly the cosmopolitan character of the age. The decorations, too, are dependent in many instances on foreign sources, but are also those employed in other media, especially those to be found in metalwork.

T'ang ceramic forms are characterized by a roundness and fullness that is often voluptuous and sometimes even frankly vulgar. There is also a tendency towards emphatic contrasts in contours, vases with narrow necks that spread widely at the lip and have round swelling bodies. Even the ordinary jar form which seems synonymous with the very name T'ang, tends to have an almost exaggerated contraction of the body towards the slightly spreading base. There is a clear liking for dynamic curves, and, except when there is deliberate imitation of similar forms in either metal or wood (Colour Plate A), the clay materials whether used for constructing on the wheel or in moulds, or for figures, are used with great boldness and with a keen appreciation of volume.

The tomb figures reflect similar preferences, but here the interest in realism is predominant. The potters' capacity to translate observation of reality into the clay figures of men, women, children and animals reached its greatest height in the first half of the T'ang. The figures have always been highly prized for this quality of realism alone, but they are also important documents of social history. The excavation of dated T'ang tombs over the last twenty or so years makes it clear that in the case of figures of women the chronology of these figures at least can be established. The women of T'ang were no less fashion conscious than they are today and the figures are revealing evidence not only of this, but also of the concepts of feminine beauty, which underwent a remarkable change between the end of the seventh century and the middle of the eighth century.

The chronology of T'ang ceramics as a whole presents very real difficulties. The main reason for this is that until recent years there has not been any archaeological work carried out on T'ang sites, and even now the number of sites of this period so far studied is small. In the past almost all the T'ang material available in whatever medium has come from ransacked tombs. Until systematic excavation is undertaken on a larger and more intensive scale than hitherto we shall remain in many instances almost totally in the dark. The Yüeh wares for instance, which are so much admired throughout the world from Japan to Egypt, are almost totally impossible to follow through the T'ang dynasty. We know the type of Yüeh produced before the T'ang at such kilns as those at Chiu-yen, and we know the later Yüeh of the tenth century, but virtually nothing of what was made during the T'ang dynasty itself until the latter part of the period sometime in the ninth century. No doubt in time it may prove possible to plot the progress of the pottery throughout the T'ang dynasty but at present the picture of development is somewhat clouded, except for a few small areas.

One of these small areas, of which some account must be included in any study of T'ang wares, is the Liao. Since the Liao inherited much from the central north Chinese tradition it fits comfortably into place as an epilogue to a splendid age.

Chapter 2

THE LEAD-GLAZED AND UNGLAZED EARTHENWARES

One of the great advantages of using lead as a flux in glaze is that it takes the addition of colouring oxides particularly well, coloured glazes being clean and usually quite brilliant. Another important advantage follows from this in as much as the brilliance of the colour, particularly the green produced by copper oxide, conceals the colour of the body. In Han times the lead-glazed wares were generally green, and far from this colour being used to imitate the patina of bronze, it was rather to hide the red earthenware body. It has to be remembered that although the potters imitated bronze shapes, they were *not* imitating the patina of 'ancient bronze' as is popularly believed. The bronzes they copied were contemporary ones, the colour of which was likely to be brown unless kept polished. When the glaze was left colourless, the appearance was of a warm amber, the glaze taking up the iron from the highly charged red body. Very occasionally the glaze was coloured with an iron oxide, producing a more positive dense brown.

The use of two colours was not normally found on a single piece and there are so far only two pieces of this kind recorded for the Han period, both of them copies of bronze *lien*,[1] which have a green central band and raised amber borders above and below. These lead glazes were confined in their use to pots intended for the tomb, and it has seemed curious that although burial practices remained virtually unchanged through the following centuries, it appeared until recently that no lead-glazed wares were included after the end of the Han dynasty until T'ang, their place being taken by dark-grey earthenware often painted with unfired pigments either directly on the body or over an applied white slip.

On present evidence the break in the tradition of lead glazing between Han and T'ang may be more apparent than real, so that it is essential to notice a number of examples between the early third century and the seventh century;

---

1. *Lien* are cylindrical vessels, usually about as high as they are wide, with a domed lid; they normally stand on three bear-shaped feet. One ceramic copy is in Tenri Ethnographical Museum in Japan, illustrated in *Sekai Tōji Zenshū* (hereafter *STZ*), 1956, Vol. 8, Pl. 13 in colour, and the other is in Boston Museum of Fine Arts.

A Polychrome lead–glazed JAR AND LID. Ht. 26.6cm (10.5in)
8th century
St. Louis City Art Gallery. See pages 14 and 26

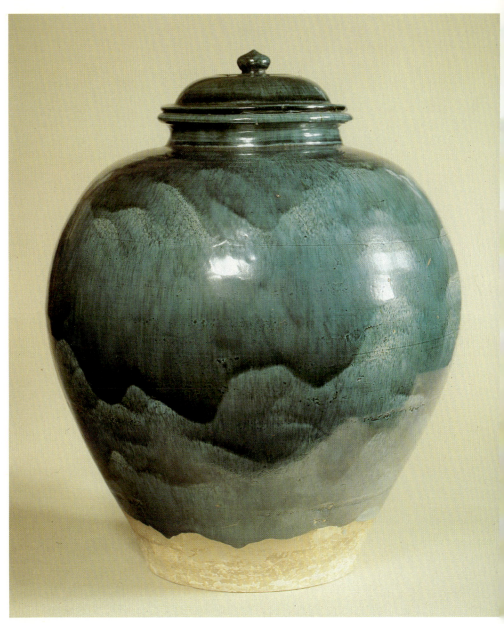

B   Blue lead-glazed JAR AND LID, the glaze having been poured on in layers. Ht. 41.1cm (16.2in)
8th century
National Trust, Ascott Collection. See page 26

1 Brown lead-glazed HORSE. Ht. 30.7 cm
(12.1 in), Length 39.5 cm (15.5 in)
From a tomb in Shansi dated to A.D. 485
2 Brown-glazed CAMEL. Ht. 31.5 cm
(12.4 in)
From the Shansi tomb dated A.D. 485

after all, four hundred years is a long time. One important instance to mention is that noted by Mizuno of greenish-brown lead-glazed tiles with red body at Yün-kang in Shansi, dating, he believed, to the latter half of the fifth century when activity at the Buddhist caves there was just beginning.[2] The second example is a wide-mouthed vase of soft red pottery with brown and green glaze in the British Museum, of uncertain date, and a third is the 'notorious lead-glazed three-colour coffin' in the British Museum. This last piece bears what Professor Watson has referred to as the 'dubious inscription' dating to the year A.D. 527.[3] Recent archaeological work has tended to reinforce the tenuous lead-glazing tradition linking Han to Sui and T'ang. Further work, especially in north China, may strengthen the connection, as it is from the more northerly region of north China that the most recent evidence has come.

In 1965 a tomb dating to A.D. 485 in the vicinity of Ta-t'ung in Shansi was discovered and excavated.[4] The tomb finds of pottery have been largely overshadowed by the very important painted lacquer panels and the sculpture in stone also found in the tomb. The pottery included a series of unglazed figures painted in the familiar red and blue unfired pigments on a white slip ground over grey earthenware. But there were also several interesting figures of sturdy little Mongolian ponies, camels and some grooms (Plates 1 and 2). The

2. *STZ* 1956, Vol. 9, p. 164, Mizuno's chapter in this work. See also the green-glazed jar in *STZ* 1976, Vol. 11, Pl. 3.
3. W. Watson, 'On T'ang soft-glazed pottery', *Percival David Foundation Colloquies on Art and Archaeology in Asia*, No. 1, 1971, p. 35. I am inclined to accept this rather curious object as genuinely of the period.
4. 'The tomb of Ssŭ-ma Chin-lung of Northern Wei at Shih-chia, Ta-t'ung, Shansi', *WW* 1972, No. 3, pp. 20–33 (in Chinese).

ponies and camels were glazed brown and the grooms green, and a couple of pieces in polychrome.[5]

The question to be asked is how does it come about that these rather realistic figures should appear in an area so remote from the main centres of pottery production, which in early times were mainly in Shensi, near Ch'ang-an, and in Honan? It seems likely that part of the answer is to be found in the very name used to describe lead-glazed wares. They are said to be *liu-li* or *po-li*, both names also meaning glass and it is significant that both names were applied by the Chinese to the lead-silicate glass that was made in north China in the Six Dynasties period.[6] The tradition of glass-making is very strong in the Ta-t'ung region and the area has for many centuries also been famous for its polychrome-glazed tiles. Joseph Needham remarks with reference to glass making that 'The art seems to have been recondite in character, and often distinctly localised so that here and there it had to be revived from time to time.'[7] As lead-silicate glass and lead-silicate glazes are so closely related it seems likely that they survived more or less alongside each other in some of the districts more remote from the old capital of Loyang in Honan. It is also worth considering the more likely explanation that lead glazing survived in lead-glazed roof-tiles, a view quite strongly expressed, with some supporting evidence, by Chiang Hsüan-t'ai in an article on ancient *liu-li*.[8]

In the course of the sixth century a number of finds from dated tombs indicate a greater continuity, examples of lead-glazed wares having come from tombs of the Northern Ch'i period in the region of An-yang in Honan.[9] In the last quarter of the sixth century and the first decade of the seventh a number of rather elaborate green-glazed vessels were made, which display a strongly westernized taste. There are several vases of large handsome proportions, the bodies of which are ornamented with applied reliefs, and one or two small cups of unusual shapes decorated in a similar fashion (Plate 3). The examples in the Ashmolean Museum in Oxford and even more the rhyton (Plates 4 and 5), although white ware, betray quite clearly their ultimate source of inspiration in the survival of late classical elements in the art of the western side of Central

5. Ibid., Pls. 12–14.
6. E. H. Schafer, *The Golden Peaches of Samarkand*, Berkeley and Los Angeles, 1963, pp. 235–7 and the notes referring to these pages.
7. *Science and Civilization in China*, Vol. IV, Pt. 1, Section 26, 'Physics', g. 5, p. 111. The whole sub-section, 'Chinese Glass Technology' also provides the most important references to the literature.
8. 'Ku-tai liu-li', 'Ancient Glass', by Chiang Hsüan-t'ai, *WW* 1969, No. 6, pp. 8–12. Also an interesting reference in Schafer, op. cit., p. 236, quoting *Hsin T'ang-shu* on temples in Burma, the tiles of which were covered with *liu-li* (Ch. 222).
9. 'Short report on the excavation of the tomb of Fang Ts'ui of Northern Ch'i at Anyang, Honan', in *WW* 1972, No. 1, pp. 47–57. These date to the period A.D. 562–4. I suspect that the plain white vases, one with a green splash on Fig. 33, were higher fired than those of earlier times and that the green splash of copper is the oxide fritted with lead to produce this colour locally in an alkaline glaze, a common practice in later times in the Ch'ang-sha material. The text refers to these vases as *tz'ŭ*, 'high-fired', and elsewhere they are referred to as porcellanous, *pan-t'ao-pan-tz'ŭ*, 'half earthenware half porcelain'.

3 Green-glazed earthenware VASE with applied moulded reliefs of jewel motifs and
   lion heads. Ht. 59.8 cm (23.5 in)
   Late 6th century
   Freer Gallery of Art

4 White-ware moulded
RHYTON with some incised
details. The lion's eyes are
glazed brown. Length 12.7 cm
(5 in)
Early T'ang, 7th century
British Museum

5 Detail of the white-ware
RHYTON showing the faces in
relief set in beaded borders

6 Brown-glazed buff earthenware VASE with cupped mouth and crazed glaze.
Ht. 22.9 cm (9 in)
Late 6th century
Victoria and Albert Museum

Asia. The use of relief heads looking out from circular frames is a feature remarkably persistent in the art to be found from Hellenistic Syria across to Central Asia, and from the second and third centuries A.D. right down into the early Islamic period in the seventh and eighth centuries.

Not all the lead-glazed wares were of this elaborate kind. There are also some very simple shapes such as the pear-shaped vase with cupped mouth similar to the one shown in Plate 6. A number of these have been recorded from tombs dating to the last decade of the sixth century.[10] They are characterized by a red body and a glaze which has often been applied in more than one layer, so that the colour is darker on the upper part of the vessel. This practice of applying the lead glaze to undecorated pieces in two or more layers was to become popular in the T'ang, and is seen at its best and most attractive in the blue and the brown-glazed jars.

It was in the Northern Ch'i period for the first time that there occurred white-bodied pieces in the tomb alongside the soft-grey earthenware. The white earthenware pieces, both vessels and figures, increased in number in Sui,

10. See *KK* 1957, No. 3, pp. 28–37. The latest date of this group of Fèng family tombs is A.D. 589. There was also a white-bodied piece with rather a bright-green glaze dashed with brownish yellow, as well as green glass in association with it.

some of them overpainted in colours and gilt, and together with these appeared porcellanous figures of large size with a clear yellowish or straw-coloured glaze (Plates 7 and 8).

In the Sui dynasty and into the early years of the T'ang the picture presented by the tomb finds is slightly confusing, but broadly may be summarized by saying that lead-glazed figures and vessels began to increase at the expense of the porcellanous ones, vessels like those found at the end of the sixth century in such tombs as those of General Chang Shêng (A.D. 595) at An-yang,[11] and of P'u Jên, also at An-yang, who died in A.D. 603.[12] From the end of Sui there were to be no more high-fired white porcellanous figures; from then on with few exceptions a whitish earthenware was used, either being painted with unfired pigments or being glazed with a thin, pale straw-coloured transparent glaze, the colour coming from the relatively low iron content of the body. The glazes were sometimes of poor fit, tending to craze and peel off. There are exceptions to such pieces as these, for example the relatively small number of tomb figures of men wearing cloaks, which have been glazed brown,[13] and of camels and riders (Plate 9).

From early in the T'ang the use of uncoloured lead glaze gradually increased and soon the practice of applying a white slip to the body was adopted. This had beneficial effects, for the excessive crazing declined and the adhesion of the glaze improved; and not only this, the colour brightened.

The most startling change came at the end of the seventh and beginning of the eighth century when polychromy was reintroduced. At first, in the seventh century, green and amber-brown together with a colourless glaze were used, but then a new, fourth colour, cobalt blue was added. The effect of all these was brilliant, and was well suited to the splendour and extravagance of the age. The earliest datable example of the use of cobalt blue is the camel carrying musicians, from the tomb dated A.D. 723 (Plate 50), an extremely elaborate one from this richly furnished tomb discovered at Sian, the modern name for Ch'ang-an, in 1957.[14] At this point attention must be drawn to the finds from the tomb of Chêng Jên-t'ai dated 664 and situated near Ch'ang-an.[15] The tomb contained a vast wealth of earthenware figures, many of them elaborately embellished with unfired pigments and gilding. There were also numerous figures, the bodies clothed in a bright green or a yellowish glaze, the faces alone being painted in unfired pigments. The most controversial find was the broken knob from a jar-lid. This is reported to be high fired and glazed white with blue splashes. Unfortunately it is necessary to accept this statement about blue with considerable caution since the Chinese word *lan* used in the report, meaning

11. *KK* 1959, No. 10, pp. 541–5 and Pls. 9–13.
12. *An-yang fa-chüeh pao-kao*, Part II, by Li Chi, 1929. Others similar to these came from the Fêng family tombs. See *KK* 1957, No. 3, pp. 28–37.
13. *STZ* 1976, Vol. 11, Pl. 131 shows two typical examples.
14. *KK* 1958, No. 1, pp. 42–52, Pls. 1–10; and illustrated in colour in *STZ* 1976, Vol. 11, Pl. 72.
15. *WW* 1972, No. 7, pp. 33–42; see fig. 13 on p. 40.

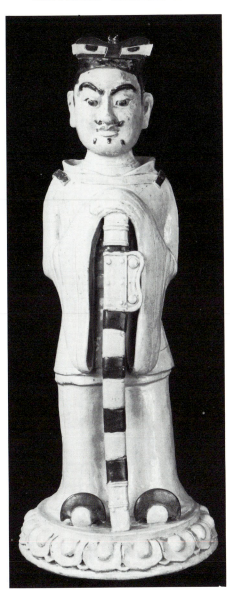 

7 TOMB GUARDIAN. Whitish stoneware with dark-brown and pale straw-coloured glazes. Ht. 72.5 cm (28.5 in) From the tomb of Chang Shêng (died 595) at Anyang

8 TOMB GUARDIAN. Pale straw-coloured glaze on a whitish body. Ht. 64 cm (25.2 in) From the tomb of Chang Shêng

blue, is also used to refer to a bright turquoise colour. If the colour was in fact a bright turquoise then the metallic oxide in a high-fired glaze would be copper and not cobalt. The fragmentary nature of the object and the ambiguity of the Chinese language does not justify the assumption that cobalt blue was already in use by this relatively early date. Indeed even in the tomb of Princess Yung-t'ai, dating to A.D. 706, the polychrome-glazed objects fail to include blue, although green, brown and white are all used.[16] The same can be said of the similarly dated tomb of Prince I-tê.[17] There are no dated tombs between those of Yung-t'ai and I-tê and the one dated A.D. 723. It should not be thought that after full polychromy was adopted that there are no monochromes, it is simply that they are far outnumbered by the gaily patterned wares. As in the Han dynasty most pieces were made specifically for burial. Nevertheless, as we shall see presently, there were some pieces which may have been made for use despite the fact that the Chinese household was amply provided with lacquer and glazed stonewares for daily use.

A major difference between Han lead glaze and that of T'ang is that in Han times the glaze was almost certainly applied in a raw state and thus was very poisonous. It also tended to display certain unsightly black specks or mottling, while in T'ang the glaze material was evidently derived from a fritted form of lead, the lead having been melted down in combination with other necessary components, such as some of the clay body material, into a glassy state which, when quenched in cold water to shatter it, is crushed and finely ground; after this it would be mixed with water ready for application. This advance in technique, which reduced the toxicity, was probably the result of a desire for colour, since it was easy to add the colouring oxide to the raw materials in much the same way as one would colour glass. The visual effect of a fritted glaze is one of brightness and transparency such as does not occur in the use of raw lead.[18] The change in technique can be deduced also from the fact that cobalt appears in China from Persia in the form of blue cabochons of *liu-li* or glass.[19] The glass cabochons were ready for use as soon as they were crushed and ground up.

In the T'ang period there remains a curious and still only partially explained fact about lead glazing. We have seen that there is a tenuous link with the Han tradition, that the technique certainly blossomed at the end of the seventh century, and that both vessels and figures were made primarily for the tomb. In 756 when the An Lu-shan rebellion broke out, soon to be followed by the Tibetan invasion of 763, T'ang China was rent apart by war and suffered

16. *WW* 1964, No. 1, p. 11 et seq.
17. *WW* 1972, No. 7, pp. 26–32.
18. In raw-glazed pieces the lead seems to be unevenly distributed, a fact revealed in X-ray studies on Islamic pottery. See U. Schultze-Frentzel and H. Salge, 'Glazes and decorating colours of Persian Islamic ceramics examined by X-radiography and transparent Seljuq glazes examined by electron-probe microanalysis', *Kunst des orients*, X, 1975, pp. 80–90.
19. R. J. Charleston, 'Glass "cakes" as raw materials and articles of commerce', *Journal of Glass Studies*, 5, 1963, pp. 54–68.

9 Green and brown lead-glazed earthenware figure of a loaded CAMEL AND RIDER. Ht. 48.3 cm (19 in), Length 39 cm (15.3 in)
Sui or early T'ang, 7th century
Royal Ontario Museum

permanent economic damage. From this time the lead-glazed tomb figures virtually disappear. As these would seem to have been made in the metropolitan areas of Ch'ang-an, the modern Sian in Shensi, and Loyang in Honan, both of which were overrun by the rebels and the Tibetans, this is scarcely surprising. What is surprising however is the persistence of small moulded vessels coloured either green and amber-brown, or blue and amber, sometimes with white and always on a heavy, very white hard body, until at least the end of the eighth century. It is this very hard, pure-white earthenware which may have been intended for domestic use.[20] Examples of bowls and small dishes are to be noted, for instance among the finds from the Yung-t'ai tomb, that are of this unusually hard type, and most pieces are rather well made and carefully finished and glazed. This seems to suggest that at least some of the practical shapes were in use to a limited extent. After the end of the eighth century lead glazing, except possibly for roof-tiles, disappears northwards ultimately to reappear in Liao pottery and at the kilns in north-east China during the late T'ang and the tenth century. At this same date too cobalt vanishes from the scene until the fourteenth century.

Lead-glazed vessels

The lead-glazed wares may conveniently be divided into two main categories: vessels and figures, the latter discussed in Chapter 3. Both are remarkably varied and owe as much to foreign influence as to the indigenous tradition, and they reflect the social and economic patterns of a relatively short but particularly colourful period.

The lead-glazed earthenware vessels are dependent in shape on both native and foreign tradition, but to some extent it may be said that a common factor, which makes them characteristically T'ang, is to be found in the swelling forms and the dynamic contours. Contrasting contours and almost extravagant roundness, expanding to the point almost of bursting are the features to make an immediate visual impact. The most characteristic shape, one owing nothing to foreign influence, is the lidded jar (Colour Plate A) with well-rounded rather high shoulders narrowing towards the bottom, but often spreading dramatically to the base, which is always flat and unglazed. Normally the monochrome-glazed examples are dipped, and the tell-tale 'swags' about two-thirds of the way down the body are a constant feature. There are exceptions to the dipping process of glazing, as for instance in the large blue-glazed jar in the Ascott Collection with the glazes evidently having been poured on in several layers with spectacular effect (Colour Plate B). The lids (and many jars lack these) are

20. This suggestion was made to me by Madeleine Paul-David with regard to the pieces from the Yung-t'ai tomb. She had the opportunity to handle these pieces when they were exhibited in Paris in 1974. In my own more recent study of similar vessels I incline to some measure of agreement. It would seem that only some of the smaller vessels are involved. Much more evidence is required before a firm conclusion can be reached.

made with precision, strongly resembling turned woodwork with a neat ridge midway between the edge and the bud-shaped knob. They are hollow inside and have a nicely made flange that fits cleanly into the mouth-rim of the jar. In polychrome examples, as we shall see, the treatment is more varied. It should be noted that the body was invariably slipped before the application of the glaze, and this goes for almost all shapes and types of the pale pinkish-white or white earthenware with lead glaze during the period. The advantages were better adhesion of the glaze and greater brilliancy in colour.

Among other popular Chinese shapes are the small, almost spherical pots of

10 JAR with amber-brown ground and applied reliefs
in green and white. Ht. 17.6 cm (6.9 in)
Early 8th century
Goto Museum, Tokyo

various kinds, some with lugs on the shoulder, some on three lion feet (Plate 10); the neck is short and straight or rolled at the rim. These like the large jars may have a flat unglazed base cleanly finished and occasionally bevelled at the edge. The shape is the culmination of a tradition going back into the fifth century.

To such purely Chinese shapes as these should be added the pleasing bowls, rounded on the lower part, and flaring in the upper part, very frequently with a small ridge marking the change in contour (Plate 11). Fundamentally this is a metallic shape, the rather hard line round the middle and the slightly spreading foot being important indications of its ancestry. Unlike the jars, the bowls normally have a neatly cut foot-ring and this, together with the base, is left bare of glaze; such pieces are always well finished. The cup or small bowl shape, another very simple form of neat finish, generally has a flat or carefully

11 White, green and brown-glazed
white earthenware BOWL. Diameter
8 cm (3.1 in)
From the tomb of Princess Yung-
t'ai, A.D. 706

12 Small white-bodied BOWL, slipped
and glazed deep blue. Diameter
10.8 cm (4.3 in)
Early 8th century
British Museum

cut concave base, and the lip may be straight or everted; only very rarely is the base bevelled at the edge (Plate 12).

A further Chinese shape is the slightly depressed globular vase with cupped mouth (Plate 13). The origins of this shape go back into the fifth century when it was made in the higher-fired earthenwares and early stonewares of Hunan, Honan and Hopei, as well as in the earlier Yüeh of northern Chekiang.[21] By the T'ang dynasty it seems to have become particularly popular so it may be found in most types of material, in bronze, earthenware, stoneware and porcellanous wares. In earthenware it is either in monochrome or in splashed polychrome; calculated decoration of the kind seen on most other types seems largely to have been avoided, although a few are recorded.

Such simple wheel-made practical shapes lie at the heart of the Chinese tradition, but running parallel are the numerous excursions into shapes which require careful construction. There are many examples of models of caskets, often on legs, innumerable small round boxes, as well as wrist-rests, which would have been built up of individually made parts luted together, besides the many small moulded pieces with decoration incorporated in the mould. Among such pieces as these are bowls in fanciful flower form or quatrefoil trays on stumpy-shaped feet (Plate 14). The variety of these less conventional shapes is considerable. At one end of the scale we may find a lamp made in the shape of a duck with its head turned back towards the oil tray on the tail (Plate 15), or the model of a memorial slab set up erect on the back of the tortoise, to a globular jar on three lion-claw cabriole legs (Plate 10).

An intermediate shape between the purely Chinese traditions and those of the more westerly regions of Asia is a tazza-like offering-tray (Plate 16), simply constructed in two parts of which sixth-century examples, some with impressed decoration in the grey body under a yellowish-olive glaze are known,

21. A good example is no. 40 in Tregear, *Catalogue of Greenwares in the Ashmolean Museum*, Oxford, 1976, which is dated to the early fifth century.

13 Depressed globular JAR
AND LID. White earthenware
with green, amber and
colourless glazes over a
white-slipped body.
Ht. 16.4 cm (6.5 in)
Early 8th century
Yamato Bunkakan

14 Fancy-shaped TRAY with
amber-brown glaze, green
and white. Diameter
40.6 cm (16 in)
Early 8th century
Tokyo National Museum

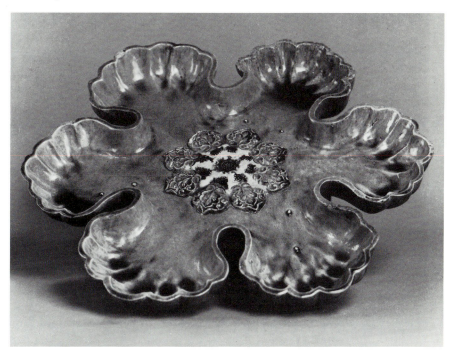

15 Moulded earthenware LAMP in the shape of a duck; amber, green and white. Ht. 7.8 cm (3 in)
8th century
City Art Museum, St. Louis

16 Earthenware TAZZA with green, brown and white glazes. Ht. 6.6 cm (2.6 in)
Early 8th century
Tokyo National Museum

one fairly recently having come from a Hupei find, but these earlier examples are of stoneware.[22]

The more usual offering-tray, either on three cabriole feet or on three ring feet, is of western Central Asian origin, being known in silver on rather tall legs with repoussé decoration.[23] A Chinese silver adaptation of the shape is in the Shōsōin.[24] In earthenware the wide central field lends itself especially well to decoration and so far as is known no monochrome example exists; the invitation to decorate seems to have been irresistible, especially with motifs which reinforce the circular character of the surface (Plate 17). In shape they may have flattened rims and a shallow well, or they may have a rounded well and everted rim.

More alien to the Chinese repertoire are a number of ewer shapes, often lavishly ornamented with applied reliefs or with decoration incorporated in the moulds from which some of these pieces are wholly constructed. The type with applied reliefs has a full rounded body with a high spreading foot, narrow neck, and a mouth usually incorporating a spout in the form of a phoenix head (Plate 18), or pinched in and resembling the classic *oinochoe*; the vessel would be held either by a simple strap or ribbed handle, or one of complicated moulded construction.

The type of ewer constructed in decorated moulds was even more novel. It was made in two halves, each half incorporating decoration and slightly flattened in the body area; the two parts were luted together so that the joint ran vertically up to the neck and spout (Plate 19). A handle, usually with

22. For example the high-footed green-glazed tray from the Pu Jên tomb find, see *WW* 1958, No. 8, p. 47.
23. V. Smirnov, *L'Argenterie orientale*, St. Petersburg, 1909, Pl. 77.
24. M. Ishida and G. Wada, *The Shōsōin, an Eighth Century Treasure House*, Tokyo, 1954, Pl. 95.

17   Earthenware OFFERING-TRAY with impressed decoration coloured green, blue,
and amber against a white ground. Diameter 25.7 cm (10.1 in)
8th century
Formerly Sotheby & Co.

decorative terminals, was then added. The spout, again in phoenix-head shape,
is blind, the only opening being through the top. As vessels of this kind were
made for the tomb, the fact that they did not pour through a proper spout was
immaterial.

The amphora shape, like the *oinochoe* type ewer, echoes the Hellenistic
survivals in the oasis states and the cities of western Central Asia (Plate 20).
The Chinese version underwent certain modifications. It was taller, rounded in
the shoulder and more tapering towards the base which was flat, while the two
handles, occasionally three, were drawn high above the level of the mouth and
then bent downward to meet the rim of the cup-shaped mouth, and the join
was in the shape of a dragon head, the rim being gripped in the jaws. Some of
these specimens are of rather hard, slightly greyish earthenware or stoneware
covered with a transparent colourless glaze. However, many are the usual

18 Earthenware EWER with applied
reliefs painted and splashed in green
and amber on a white ground.
Ht. 34.1 cm (13.4 in)
Early 8th century
Private collection in Japan

19 Moulded EWER made in two
vertical halves with an added
handle, with green, amber and white
glazes. Ht. 22.1 cm (8.7 in)
Early 8th century
Tokyo National Museum

pinkish-white earthenware with the more decorative polychrome glazes, and a few also ornamented with applied reliefs (Plate 21).

The tall bottle-shaped vases with long neck, high spreading foot and near-spherical body seem only to occur in polychrome (Plate 22). The shape probably has a metal ancestry, as suggested by the frequent use of a small raised rib or collar at the junction of the neck and body, but the antecedent is less easily traced than in the case of the *oinochoe* and amphora.

Finally among the vessels are the deep cups, round, hexagonal or octagonal with an everted lip, ring handle and a sharp angled contraction to the small foot (Plate 23). The shape can be traced through contemporary metalwork of Chinese manufacture to imported examples from either Sogdia or Khorezm on the western side of Central Asia.[25] The large numbers of Sogdian merchants in

25. M. Medley, *Metalwork and Chinese Ceramics* (PDF Monograph No. 2), 1972, pp. 5–6.

C OFFERING-TRAY; blue, green and amber on a white ground. Diameter 18.1cm (7.1in)
8th century
Honolulu Academy of Arts. See page 41

D SEATED LADY with a mirror; polychrome lead glazes on a slipped body.
Ht. 30.5cm (12in)
8th century
Victoria and Albert Museum. See page 46

20 Whitish earthenware AMPHORA with a very pale straw-coloured
transparent glaze. Ht. 50 cm (19.7 in)
7th–8th century
Present whereabouts not known

the two capitals during the period would account very easily for the introduction of this shape, which ultimately has a Mediterranean origin.

These then are the major shapes made in earthenware with which one quickly becomes familiar. But what about the decoration? And how was it done? It is to decoration that it is now necessary to turn before discussing the figures, and remember that the same techniques and styles of decoration are to be found on both vessels and figures.

Decorative techniques

The techniques used in decoration include simple splashing of coloured glazes, glaze painting, impressing, moulding and the use of moulded reliefs. There is one other technique which is more complex and this is the use of wax resist in the creation of designs. Some or all of these techniques may be used together. However, painting with coloured glazes on a plain surface is not as a rule combined with other techniques.

The use of splashing was always popular probably because it was easily done. Because of the low viscosity of the lead glaze it ran down on a sloping or vertical surface producing a streaked effect often without decorative logic, but sometimes undeniably attractive. In many instances a colourless transparent glaze is applied to the slip-covered body, and on this the coloured spots and splashes, when on a flat surface, tend to run or form untidy blots. The colour combinations are varied from one piece to the next.

Painting in coloured glazes, if well done, can be very effective, especially when bold, broad brush strokes are used to form checker or chevron patterns, or simple floral designs. On dishes the colours, white, green, and amber-brown or yellow, smudge into each other to some extent but not so much as to destroy the design (Plate 24). Curiously enough blue seems not to have been used in this style. On large jars there is inevitably a strong tendency for the colours to run down in unsightly streaks, and the only way to avoid this is to leave a narrow unglazed area between each colour, or to paint a line of wax resist as a separation barrier.

The use of the wax-resist technique to produce spots and florets is peculiar and would certainly have been almost impossible to accomplish were it not for the use of the white slip.[26] As noted earlier the white slip helps glaze adherence. The slip has a much higher silica content than the earthenware body so that it is possible, if the firing temperature is high enough, to achieve a slight gloss. In such examples as the offering-tray in the Victoria and Albert Museum and the lidded jar in the British Museum, the hot wax has been spotted directly on to the slip; the other coloured glaze or glazes have then been applied and have left the wax spots showing as the glaze pulled away from them (Plates 25 and 26). In the firing the wax becomes volatile leaving the highly siliceous white slip to

26. *STZ* 1976, Vol. 11. Sato Masahiko discusses this briefly on pp. 234–5.

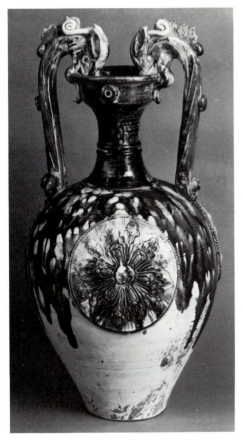

21 Earthenware AMPHORA with applied
reliefs painted and splashed with green
and amber glazes. Ht. 47.4 cm (18.6 in)
Early 8th century
Tokyo National Museum

22 Earthenware VASE with applied
reliefs glazed green and white.
Ht. 30.5 cm (12 in)
Early 8th century
British Museum

23 Earthenware CUP with
handle and impressed
decoration under a warm
amber-brown glaze.
Ht. 6.7 cm (2.6 in)
7th–8th century
British Museum

24   Earthenware DISH on a high foot. The body slipped in white and then painted
in green, amber and colourless glazes to resemble the tie and dye techniques of
textile decoration. Diameter 36.8 cm (14.5 in)
Early 8th century
British Museum

achieve a slight gloss. Larger areas do not lend themselves to this treatment,
which is its limitation. Such areas need to be painted separately with a
colourless glaze over the slip so as to fire to clean white. It is noticeable that the
white that occurs with the wax-resist technique is always rather dull and dirty.

The combination of glaze painting with impressing is the most favoured
treatment for the flat surfaces such as are presented by offering-trays, dishes
and wrist-rests. The gutters between the elements in an impressed decoration
to some extent inhibit the tendency towards smudging, but it will depend upon
how well the painting of the elements has been executed. There are some
instances in which two colours have been laid down side by side without a
gutter, and then the colours naturally spill over and this seems a deliberate
choice.

Moulded decoration is either included in the structure of the mould in
which a vessel is made, as in some of the fanciful shapes such as shell-like

E Caparisoned lead-glazed HORSE. Ht. 44.1cm (17.4in), Length 54.6cm (21.5in)
8th century
Victoria and Albert Museum. See page 56

F Whitish earthenware HORSE, slipped and transparently glazed, and splashed with blue.
Ht. 29.8cm (11.7in)
8th century
British Museum. See page 56

vessels or duck-shaped lamps (Plate 27), or it may be an applied element. The applied moulded decoration only occurs on vases, ewers and jars. In some cases quite a number of different patterns are used and distributed in a carefully planned manner over the surface. The use of these elements is normally combined with splashing or glaze painting, the reliefs sometimes being dabbed with different colours against a white or some other coloured ground (Plate 28). Such painted parts invariably become streaked.

The decorations

The decorations can be divided up into three groups, each one having a different origin. The heads under which they may be most satisfactorily grouped are textiles, jewellery and silverwork.

25 OFFERING-TRAY in green, brown and white glaze on a white-slipped body.
   Diameter 38.1 cm (15 in)
   8th century
   Victoria and Albert Museum

28 JAR AND LID with applied reliefs painted with green, blue and amber, the
green and blue flowing down into the transparent colourless glaze over the
white-slipped pale-pinkish earthenware body. Ht. 24.5 cm (9.6 in)
8th century
Seikado Foundation, Tokyo

26 (*opposite above*) JAR AND LID painted in green and white with a textile style of
decoration. Ht. 25 cm (9.8 in)
8th century
British Museum

27 (*opposite below*) Duck-shaped earthenware VESSEL, moulded and painted with
green, yellow and pale-brown glazes. Ht. 24 cm (9.4 in)
8th century
Seikado Foundation, Tokyo

29 JAR AND LID painted
in the style of a tie and
dye textile.
Ht. 20.5 cm (8 in)
8th century
British Museum

The textile origins of the boldly painted, large-scale designs, such as those of
the type represented by the high-footed tray in the British Museum, illustrated
in Plate 24, are not far to seek in the contemporary textiles that have come
down in Central Asian and Shōsōin material. The smaller scale decorations with
florets and stripes with dots (Plate 29), using the wax-resist technique,
similarly develop out of the textile tradition with its immediate antecedents in
the tie and die silks and wax-stencilled resist designs of the type found over the
last twenty years in Central Asia, particularly in the Turfan area at Astana.[27]
    The dependence on jewellery is to be seen primarily in the use of relief
elements, and is particularly obvious in those pieces which have beaded
borders.[28] Among the earliest examples of this type are the green-glazed vase in
the Freer (Plate 3), and the white stoneware bowl on a high foot dating to A.D.
667 (Plate 60). The style was taken over into the polychrome lead-glazed
tradition and is seen in the great range of vases, jars and ewers of the eighth
century. The derivation is very obvious in most cases, but there is a tendency to
modify, and in modification to move towards the use of naturalistic elements,

27. *Hsin-chiang ch'u-t'u wên-wu* (Cultural relics unearthed in Sinkiang), Peking, 1975, Pl. 159,
and *Ssŭ-ch'ou chih lu* (The Silk Road, textiles from Han to T'ang), Peking, 1972, Pls. 51–2.
28. Note that a similar use of applied reliefs is common on the Buddhist clay figures in
Fondukistan. A seventh-century date is usually accorded to these and the idea of using such
reliefs on pots may well derive from this region. See F. M. Rice and B. Rowland, *Art in
Afghanistan*, London, 1971, Pls. 149–56.

such as prancing and galloping horses, sometimes with mounted archers, lions, and in one instance a small slave madly trying to grasp a hunting dog resembling the modern Afghan hound. Applied decoration of this kind is frequently found on the horses and camels, where harness-straps are embellished with 'metal' mounts (Plate 30).[29]

It is almost certainly silver with traced decoration that is the source for the impressed designs on the offering-trays, dishes and wrist-rests. But many of these designs belong to the common vocabulary of the age and are also found in painted panels and ceilings. In the pottery examples the repetitions of the same designs on numerous trays and dishes would be monotonous save for the

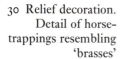

30 Relief decoration.
Detail of horse-
trappings resembling
'brasses'

potter's obvious delight in playing with his colour patterns. The design shown on the tray in the Freer Gallery is known in at least seven other examples, every one different in the arrangement of the colours and in some cases of the background itself, two of them being of the dappled type and one of these two with a glaze-painted rim (Colour Plate C and Plates 31 to 33).[30]

Without this kind of variety T'ang polychrome would undoubtedly become very boring, but the true artist can impart liveliness by creating different colour patterns which tend subtly to produce different aesthetic responses through the varying colour rhythms. In the case of the British Museum example it is important to emphasize that the whole design is made up from a single unit which is impressed into the soft clay. The design is thus not limited to use on

29. Examples of gilt-bronze harness-ornaments were found in the tombs of both Princess Yung-t'ai and Prince I-tê. See *WW* 1964, No. 1, p. 11 et seq., and *WW* 1972, No. 7, p. 26 et seq.
30. Trays with this design with differing colours are in the Victoria and Albert Museum; Museum of Fine Arts, Boston; Tokyo National Museum and a private collection in Japan.

33 OFFERING-TRAY with the same colours, varied in the centre and with a dark-
blue surround. Diameter 18.1 cm (7.1 in)
8th century
British Museum

31 (*opposite above*) OFFERING-TRAY in blue, green and amber on a white ground.
Diameter 28.5 cm (11.2 in)
8th century
Freer Gallery of Art

32 (*opposite below*) OFFERING-TRAY in the same colours with a dappled ground.
Diameter 38.1 cm (15 in)
8th century
Victoria and Albert Museum

pieces of one size only and in fact this one occurs on another larger tray surrounded by elaborate stylized clouds, each one individually impressed round the central theme.[31]

In concluding this section on the lead-glazed vessels it is significant to note that nearly all the T'ang polychrome wares in Western collections came out of China in the 1920s and 1930s, a time when the tombs around Loyang in Honan were being rifled. It is also a startling fact that in none of the tombs excavated in the Sian area in recent years have any offering-trays, ewers or vases of the types described here so far been found. Where the material was made is still largely unknown, Kung-hsien not far from Loyang being so far the only kiln site on which polychrome-glazed earthenware has been excavated.[32]. The questions that follow are obvious and we can only wait patiently for more excavation of dated tombs located in these two areas to discover whether they are a local manifestation or not. From the dated tombs in both areas so far tomb figurines have been the predominant kind of pottery.

31. One illustrated in colour *STZ*, vol. 11 (1976), Col. Pl. 59.
32. Fêng Hsien-ming, 'Honan Kung-hsien ku-yao chih t'iao-cha chi-yao' (Summary investigation of the Kung-hsien kiln site), *WW* 1959, No. 3, pp. 56–8.

Chapter 3

LEAD-GLAZED AND UNGLAZED
EARTHENWARE FIGURES

The popularity of earthenware tomb figures goes back to at least as early as the
Han dynasty, and they constitute social documents as important for T'ang as
they do for the Han period. The production of figures continued all through
the centuries following the Han, but after the end of Han, the majority were
unglazed grey earthenware, painted in unfired pigments. The Ta-t'ung tomb,
that of Ssǔ-ma Ching-lung, dated to A.D. 485, is at present exceptional in
having not only monochrome-glazed figures but polychrome ones as well.[1] By
the end of the following century both glazed and unglazed figures are found
side by side in the same tomb, and so in the Sui and T'ang dynasties it is
virtually impossible to deal with them separately. There are suggestive
differences in some cases between glazed and unglazed figures which would
seem to indicate different centres of manufacture.

The chronology of the tomb figures is necessarily dependent in the first
instance on dated tomb finds, and we are relatively fortunate now in having
such evidence for the most important period, from the end of the sixth to the
middle of the eighth century, after which figures both glazed and unglazed
almost totally disappear. With about half a dozen dated tombs between A.D. 589
and 748 we are able, using the relevant material from them, to combine
archaeologically dated material with stylistic analysis. This may sound as
though all problems are solved in lead-glazed wares between the late sixth and
mid-eighth century. Unfortunately this is not the case since while in human
figures women's fashions change, and patterns of armour *may* change, mens'
fashions barely seem to, and animals do not enter into the picture at all, nor do
the fabulous creatures. Nevertheless, with human figures some kind of scheme
can be constructed, always bearing in mind the fact that the relative number of
women's figures is small compared with Chinese and foreign men's figures, and
that it is largely on the figures of women, because of the changing fashion in
dress and hair-styles, that some kind of chronology may have to be based to
bridge the gaps between the dated tombs.

1. *WW* 1972, No. 3, pp. 20–33.

Human figures

The earthenware figurines fall into two main categories, the Chinese and the foreigner. It is of some interest that in the earlier part of our period the Chinese figures tend to outnumber those reflecting foreign origins and that glazed and unglazed figures are fairly evenly divided. As indicated above the figures constitute valuable social documents, the full value of which still remains to be exploited against the historical background.

If we look at the women in this context first, together with the methods of construction, we find that the women are normally seen engaged in duties of waiting-maids or musicians and dancers and only rarely in more sporting pursuits such as riding and polo playing (Plates 34 and 35). A small number cannot be classified as to status, as for instance those figures seen seated on stools apparently occupied with the exigencies of the toilet (Colour Plate D).

The earliest group of figures, from the tomb of Chang Shêng at Anyang, dated A.D. 595, is a small orchestra of seated women.[2] Each figure is established on a square base, fairly roughly moulded up to the shoulders. The arms and hands are added in their appropriate positions, the hands being simplified to suit the character of the material. The musical instruments are remarkably accurate models of those currently in use. The heads, all identical, have clearly been constructed in moulds, and so made that they may be slotted into the top of the roughly moulded bodies to suit the performance on the instrument each figure holds. The varied angle at which the head is adjusted in each case imparts both realism and expression such as would otherwise be lacking. Obviously speed of production to fulfil any special order was here a consideration. This holds true throughout the history of the tomb figures of the Sui and T'ang periods.

The unglazed figures from this tomb, which are mainly standing ones are similarly treated but are slightly more dumpy, perhaps because of difficulties in handling the clay, and without the rectangular bases on which to stand. This too was to be the normal treatment of standing figures, although some, both men and women, may have a shaped base to ensure stability.

In late Sui or early T'ang most of the figures are glazed with a virtually colourless transparent glaze on a whitish body, the beginning of a long tradition. In proportions they are conceived as slim, with long roughly rectangular heads, the faces being moulded very simply, the salient eyes, nose and mouth created without undue emphasis.

The progress of the seventh century until about A.D. 664 is difficult to plot, but clearly the method of construction had been established and the concept of feminity was seen as relatively slender and elegant. The figures, which can be dated satisfactorily up to the beginning of the eighth century, all display this characteristic. They are tall, elegant, and simply dressed with the exception of a

2. *KK* 1959, No. 10, pp. 541.

34 (*above left*) Seated earthenware FIGURE, unglazed and painted with unfired
pigments. Ht. 16.5 cm (6.5 in)
Late 7th or early 8th century
Barlow Collection, Sussex University

35 (*above right*) Tall earthenware FIGURE OF A SERVANT GIRL, slipped and
transparently glazed. Ht. 25.8 cm (10.1 in)
Late 7th century
Barlow Collection, Sussex University

few ceremonially dressed acting figures. However, by the end of the seventh
century the heads have become more ovoid, and while the body was often
glazed, the face was more usually left unglazed and realistically painted in
unfired pigments.

The finds in the tomb of Princess Yung-t'ai dating to A.D. 706,[3] when she was
reburied with full honours, indicate a similar style in elegance and facial
treatment, but by the end of the first quarter of the eighth century change had
set in. The heads are larger and rounder, the cheeks fuller, and the hair-style is
less tightly controlled, beginning to resemble that current in Europe in the first

3. *WW* 1964, No. 1, p. 11 et seq.

decade of the twentieth century with the bun on top of the head, but pushed farther forward. The bodies are still comparatively slim, but with added width on the shoulder, and the figure tends to lean a little heavily one way or another (Plates 36 and 37). The heads, as usual, are made in similar moulds and set into the bodies at angles which impart expression, while the arms and hands are positioned with some variety. The placing of hands, angling of the head and the use of coloured glazes (or pigments as appropriate) give just sufficient diversity to moderate the inevitable monotony of mass-production objects.

By the time of the death of Wu Shou-chung in 748 the progression towards the massive, opulent and heavy was complete. From this tomb in the modern village of Kao-lou-ts'un just outside Sian came a number of weighty-looking figures, both glazed and unglazed. The women are dressed in long robes with almost unbroken lines, and stand one foot a little forward with a slight twist in the body, and with the head inclined to left or right (Plates 39 and 40). The faces are fat, heavily brooding and vacuous while the hair-style is an exaggeration of the examples of the first quarter of the century. The faces are painted with flesh tones, rouged cheeks, red lips and marvellously curved, slender black eyebrows.[4]

Among the unglazed figures of this and the preceding period are a number of very soft red earthenware ones of rather smaller size. These are slipped in white and sometimes painted. They form a minor group and seem to represent another centre of production. They have been recorded from a tomb in Shensi dated A.D. 664 and differ both on account of size and the simplicity of their construction, which is solid in all but a very few instances. Examples of rather larger pieces, which are uncommon, are some polo-players, the women dressed as men (Plate 41).[5] It was quite normal for women to dress as men for riding at

4. See figures from the tomb of Wu Shou-chung, d. 748, *WW* 1955, No. 7, pp. 103-9.
5. A group in the Nelson Gallery of Art Collection, Kansas City.

---

36 (*opposite above*) Two earthenware FIGURES OF STANDING WOMEN in polychrome-glazed clothes, the details of the faces picked out in unfired red, pink and black, the hair painted black. Ht. left 42 cm (16.5 in), right 45 cm (17.7 in)
2nd quarter 8th century
From a tomb near Loyang, Honan

37 (*opposite left*) Standing FIGURE OF A WOMAN, the clothes glazed dark blue and yellow, the face painted in flesh tones with black eyebrows and eyes, and white floret beauty-marks on the cheeks. Ht. 41 cm (16.1 in)
8th century
Yamato Bunkakan

38 (*opposite right*) Seated FIGURE OF A WOMAN playing the clappers. The upper part of the robe painted in blue, brown, yellow and colourless glazes; the head painted in unfired pigments; black hair. Ht. 32 cm (12.6 in)
2nd quarter 8th century
Museum of Far Eastern Antiquities, Stockholm

39 Standing FIGURE OF A WOMAN in
red earthenware covered in white
slip. Ht. 45.7 cm (17.9 in)
Mid 8th century
Victoria and Albert Museum

40 Standing FIGURE OF A WOMAN
with a pet dog. Reddish earthenware
covered in white slip. Ht. 35.2 cm
(13.8 in)
Mid 8th century
Tokyo National Museum

41 Unglazed earthenware FIGURE OF A WOMAN ON HORSEBACK. The figures covered in slip and painted in unfired pigments. Length 32.7 cm (12.8 in), Ht. 25.4 cm (10 in)
Late 7th or early 8th century
Rietberg Museum, Zurich

this time and it was also a popular quirk of fashion in the two capital cities of Ch'ang-an and Loyang.

The figures of men are a great deal more varied than those of women including as they do many examples of foreigners. But even among figures which can be identified as specifically Chinese there is much variation as regards representation. Some are large, handsome, courtly guardian figures, among them a few elaborately painted unglazed figures, others are rather carefully polychrome-glazed figures, the heads painted with unfired pigments. These are static and generally sombre in expression, with hands clasped in their sleeves at waist level (Plate 42).

There are many figures of warriors in heavy breast-plated armour, some very remarkable examples of large size having come from the tomb dated A.D. 664 of Chêng Jên-t'ai.[6] Some figures from this tomb were covered with a pale straw-coloured glaze and then elaborately painted in unfired red, green, blue, white, and with black, especially for facial detail, very similar to the one illustrated (Plate 43). To these colours was added gilding. Figures of warriors not unnaturally often include foreigners, many of whom took service with the Chinese nobility as well as with the army, and they may be depicted either

6. *STZ*, 1976, Vol. 11, Pl. 32, a figure 72 cm (28.3 in) in height and in marvellous condition.

43 a & b Glazed WARRIOR GUARDIAN overpainted with polychrome unfired
pigments. Ht. 73.2 cm (28.8 in)
c. A.D. 664
Royal Ontario Museum

42 (*opposite*) Unglazed courtly GUARDIAN FIGURE painted in unfired pigments.
Ht. 88.9 cm (35 in)
Late 7th century
Victoria and Albert Museum

standing alone or mounted on chargers. The unglazed figures from the tomb of Prince I-tê, dated to A.D. 706, include an admirable series of unglazed mounted figures, the horses armoured and wearing gold head-frontals. In this tomb there were also polychrome-glazed figures of attendants of various kinds, a falconer for instance, and hunting figures equipped with bows, and one splendid figure of a mounted archer in the act of drawing his bow at a bird overhead.[7] A similar range of figures was found in the tomb of the Princess Yung-t'ai, of the same date, with among the hunting figures a heavily bearded Central Asian, bare to the waist with elaborately modelled swelling muscles on

44 Unglazed MOUNTED FIGURE of a Central Asian. Ht. 32 cm (12.6 in) From the tomb of Princess Yung-t'ai dated A.D. 706

the arms and body, and another mounted figure with a hunting dog (Plates 44 and 45).

It was very fashionable in the seventh and eighth centuries to employ foreign grooms, and the variety of racial types to be found among these figures of tomb attendants is remarkable (Plate 46). They include Central Asians such as Khorezmians, Sogdians, Uighurs and Turks, men from Tocharistan, and from even farther west, figures with Iranian or even Caucasian features.[8] All these tend to wear their native dress, so that the hats, coats, boots and shoes all give

7. *WW* 1964, No. 1, Pl. 3, nos. 1 and 2.
8. J. G. Mahler, *The Westerners among the Figurines of T'ang Dynasty China*, Rome, 1959.

clues to the origins of the inspiration. With about a quarter of a million foreigners in and around the capital, Ch'ang-an, out of a total population of around two million in the early eighth century it is hardly surprising to find all kinds of racial types depicted. Nor were warriors, huntsmen and grooms the only ones to be represented. Musicians, merchants, pedlars, dancers and acrobats are found as well as foreigners at their leisure feeding their pet birds or taking them out for an airing, thus adapting themselves to the customs of the land of their adoption (Plate 47).

The dating of the male figures is made more difficult as the result of the

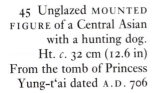

45 Unglazed MOUNTED
FIGURE of a Central Asian
with a hunting dog.
Ht. *c.* 32 cm (12.6 in)
From the tomb of Princess
Yung-t'ai dated A.D. 706

introduction of so many foreigners into the repertory. It is really only the essentially Chinese figures which in any way follow the trend towards the weight and voluptuous curves that we have already seen in the women. Unfortunately there are very few such figures and most of these are of the unglazed type, slipped in white and then painted.

In the majority of cases the modelling of the male figures is much more realistic and vigorous than that of the female figures, reflecting the more active role that most of them played in the life of the capital. This is not to say that the figures of the women lack realism or liveliness, but rather that the rhythms in the modelling are softer and the movement more leisurely and subdued.

46 Unglazed FIGURE OF A FOREIGN
GROOM. Ht. 35.6 cm (14 in)
Early 8th century
Victoria and Albert Museum

47 Unglazed FIGURE OF A FOREIGNER
with his pet bird. Ht. 18.3 cm (7.2 in)
8th century
British Museum, Seligman Bequest

48 (*opposite above*) Polychrome-glazed loaded BACTRIAN CAMEL. Ht. 88.9 cm
(35 in)
Early 8th century
Asian Art Museum of San Francisco

49 (*opposite below*) Dark-brown-glazed HORSE. Ht. 70.2 cm (27.6 in)
8th century
Chicago Art Institute

Animal figures

The other figures found representing facets of daily life are the horses, camels
and oxen. Of these the horses are perhaps the best known and most admired
(Colour Plates E and F, Plate 49). The faithfulness of portrayal, whatever the
size, is the outstanding feature. The harnessing may be minimal with no more
than a saddle-cloth or simple saddle, or indeed none at all, or be the most
elaborately ornamented bridling with moulded mounts and hanging horse-
'brasses' (Plate 49) mirroring the gilt-bronze ones in use at the time, examples

50 CAMEL AND
ORCHESTRA.
Elaborately polychrome
glazed. Ht. 58.4 cm
(22.9 in)
From the tomb of
Hsien-yü T'ing-hui
dated A.D. 723

of which were found in the tombs of both Princess Yung-t'ai and Prince I-tê.[9]
The modelling of the smaller horses is kept simple, the animals being
constructed in moulds and the parts carefully luted together and the joints
smoothed over. Larger ones must have required much more careful treatment
with very fine modelling, the heads and the area of the saddle receiving great
attention as to detail.

One peculiarity should be noticed, to which there is only very rare exception.
It is that the horse's head either looks straight forward, or is turned to the left.
For some so far unexplained reason the turn of the head is almost never to the
right. Even among the great host of horses and riders in the tomb of Prince I-tê
there appear to be only two or three examples of horses with the head slightly
inclined to the right.

This is a feature also to be noted among the camels. The camel, of the
Bactrian species, is next in popularity to the horse among the animals
represented among the tomb figures. It has been suggested, perhaps with good
reason, that as camels were beasts of burden their presence in the tomb was an
indication that the human occupant had large commercial interests. Be this as it
may, it is clear from the tomb evidence in the Ch'ang-an region that splendid

9. See above, Chapter 2, footnote 29.

Bactrian camels, loaded or unloaded, have been found in the richest tombs, such as the undated and uninscribed one at Ch'ang-p'u, found in 1959, as well as in the royal interment of Yung-t'ai. The beasts are treated with the same attention to detail as the horses, and the two most remarkable carry not any normal burden, but bands of musicians, one having come from the very important tomb of Hsien-yü T'ing-hui, dated 723 (Plate 50).[10] The one with the Central Asian men musicians bears a strong resemblance to the music-party which is painted on the plectrum of the *p'i-p'a* in the Shōsōin, which must be about the same date.[11]

Oxen and animals of the farmyard make up the rest of the repertory, and except for a few oxen about 26 or 30 centimetres (10.2 or 11.8 inches) high, most of the animals are small, cocks and hens, dogs, sheep, geese and ducks. The majority are unglazed, but when they are glazed they tend to be a suitable amber-brown, although a few oxen are more decoratively treated with splashes of green on a creamy ground and one or two are similarly treated with blue splashes.

10. Tomb of Hsien-yü T'ing-hui dated A.D. 723, *KK* 1958, No. 1, pp. 42–52.
11. M. Ishida and G. Wada, *The Shōsōin; an Eighth Century Treasure House*, Tokyo, 1954, Col. Pl. 3.

51 Polychrome-glazed figure of CH'I-T'OU with animal head.
Ht. 117 cm (46 in)
8th century
Tokyo National Museum

52 Polychrome-glazed figure of a CH'I-T'OU with semi-human head painted in unfired pigments.
Ht. 37.5 cm (14.7 in)
8th century
Minneapolis Institute of Arts

Rather different from any of the foregoing are the fabulous beasts and guardians of which there is a large number. These fall into two main groups and are generally massive, running anything from 55 centimetres (21.6 inches) high to 117 centimetres (46 inches) or even more.

One group comprises the fabulous beast, the Ch'i-t'ou, a fearsome creature with a fanged-lion or semi-human face in which the eyes bulge, teeth are bared and from whose head sprout horns and crests like flames or huge cockscombs (Colour Plate G, Plates 51 and 52). The body is that of an animal, sometimes cloven hoofed, sometimes provided with lion's paws. Large decoratively treated wings spring out from the top of the forequarters and curve upwards. The Ch'i-t'ou was regarded as the one who kept evil spirits tied down in one place. Stories about these strange beasts reach back into Han Taoist literature, but the tradition seems to have been given representational form only from about the sixth century.

Allied to this weird animal is the Fang-hsiang, which also would seem to have stemmed from the popular Taoism of the Han dynasty. Even at the time figures of them seem to have been buried in the tomb to ward off evil spirits and frighten away sickness. In the course of the intervening centuries Buddhism was widely adopted and the Fang-hsiang and the four Buddhist Dvarapala, Heavenly Kings, seem to have become merged into a fabulous crested semi-human being with bulging eyes, furiously gaping mouth and massive powerful arms and legs. Usually depicted in T'ang times trampling on a dwarf or an animal, the Fang-hsiang is closer to Buddhist than Taoist iconography (Plate 53).

Often gorgeously apparelled in elaborate semi-military clothes and birdlike head-dress, they may once have flourished swords, halberds or spears in their upraised right hands. When polychrome glazed, the faces, and often the hands, are left unglazed and then painted with reddish pigment and the faces adorned with whiskers (Plate 54).

These two types of figures, the Ch'i-t'ou and Fang-hsiang, came together in T'ang and have been found, two pairs of each within the tomb. They must have been very costly, on account of their size and the enormous difficulty in ensuring that they did not collapse in the firing, whether unglazed or glazed. They made great demands on the potters not only in the modelling, but also in the decoration. Despite endeavours on the glazed figures to keep the different colours apart, the glazes inevitably ran badly in the firing and the splashing and streaking is considerable. Nevertheless they form a striking series not to occur again in later centuries. Lion figures, often of great ferocity, form another group with affiliations to Buddhism. These are generally polychrome glazed and

---

53 (*opposite*) Unglazed figure of FANG-HSIANG painted with unfired pigments and
touches of gold. Ht. 47.6 cm (18.7 in)
8th century
British Museum

54 Figure of FANG-HSIANG
painted in polychrome glazes,
the face in unfired pigments.
Ht. 90 cm (35.4 in)
8th century
Victoria and Albert Museum

rarely of any great size. They are vigorously modelled and have a similar liveliness to that of other animal figures (Colour Plate H, Plates 55 and 56).

The other group of fabulous beasts consists of standing or squatting figures, generally unglazed, of animal-headed human beings who represent what is known as the Chinese zodiac, more correctly named the Twelve Animals of the Duodenary Cycle. Each animal is supposed to exercise an influence, according to its own attributes over the hour, day or year appropriate to it. The usage is not native to China, having been introduced effectively only in the T'ang dynasty. It originates in a northern Tartar tradition, perhaps in the Kirghiz territory of modern Outer Mongolia.

The figures appear for the first time among the tomb furnishings in the T'ang period and are found not only in China but also in Korea. They became more common in the post-T'ang period, achieving their greatest popularity in the late thirteenth and fourteenth centuries.

55 White, green and brown-glazed
    earthenware LION.
    Ht. 27.7 cm (10.9 in)
    First half of 8th century
    Eisei Foundation

56 Brown and green-glazed earthenware
    LION.
    Ht. 20.8 cm (8.2 in)
    First half of 8th century
    Seikado Foundation

One particularly good group of these figures was found in Hunan at Hsiang-yü, much farther south than the glazed figures normally occur.[12] This would seem to suggest that the appeal of the duodenary cycle to which they belong is associated with Taoist beliefs and popular superstition of a kind less commonly seen in the north in the more strongly Buddhist society of Loyang and Ch'ang-an.

It is possibly the most important aspect of all the glazed figures, with the exception of this one group, that they are more closely related to the metropolitan and Buddhist attitudes than to the magical aspects of rural beliefs and a pattern of behaviour governed by superstitions or shamanistic beliefs of the local farming communities. Whatever the difference between them both in some measure survived, but the gorgeous polychrome-glazed wares occur only intermittently after the middle of the eighth century, ceasing completely in the Ming dynasty.

12. *KK* 1957, No. 3, p. 37 et seq. See also *WW* 1972, No. 11, pp. 48–9 and the nine from the set illustrated inside the back cover.

Chapter 4
NORTHERN HIGH-FIRED WARES

As an introduction to the study of the high-fired wares of north China in the T'ang dynasty, it is helpful to look at the earlier material produced during the latter part of the Six Dynasties period, from about the end of the fifth century, so as to gain a better overall view. It is particularly important to do so because the evidence from both kiln sites and tombs in the T'ang itself is so meagre that we are forced to depend on style, and to a limited extent on the technological development. The problem is exacerbated by the terminology employed in Chinese archaeological reports, which makes no distinction between leadless and lead-glazed earthenwares, and when higher temperatures are used we do not know whether specific pieces are alkaline glazed or feldspathically glazed.[1] Such refinement has still to be achieved, and the nearest yet reached was in a recent report which included the description *pan-tz'ŭ-pan-t'ao*, 'half high-fired, half low-fired',[2] and this in some contexts might justify the translation 'porcellanous' but it does not get us very far. Despite these drawbacks if we go back before the T'ang, the evolution can be outlined reasonably well.

The developing technology of north China becomes significant in the late fifth century, and gradually grows in importance in the course of the sixth century. In the south-east in the late fifth century, the greenware, or early Yüeh type,[3] was technically the most advanced and sophisticated stoneware, enjoying a reputation it never lost. The very hard grey-bodied ware was influential and potters in the north were stimulated to renewed efforts as time passed to produce something comparable, if not better.

The first indication of a new type of ware is to be found among the pots in a tomb in northern Hupei, dated by inscription to A.D. 485, and reported in 1965.[4] The vessel is a large jar with ovoid body, high spreading foot, long neck flaring to the lip and surmounted by a domed lid; on the shoulder are four clay loops. The decoration is elaborately carved and incised with formalized scrolls

---

1. Leadless glazes are primarily alkaline; if significantly high in feldspar, then they may be termed feldspathic, and if exceptionally high in vegetable ash they may be termed ash glazes.
2. *KKHP* 1973, No. 1.
3. See below, p. 101 et seq.
4. *KK* 1965, No. 4, p. 183, Pl. 3, fig. 3.

G (*opposite*) Polychrome lead-glazed
CH'I-T'OU or EARTH SPIRIT.
Ht. 95.3 cm (37.5in)
8th century
Minneapolis Institute of Art. See page 60

H (*above*) Green and white lead-glazed
LION. Ht. 25.6cm (10in)
7th–8th century
British Museum. See page 62

I Grey stoneware JAR with applied reliefs. Ht. 38.3cm (15in)
Second half of 6th century
Ashmolean Museum. See page 66

57 Grey stoneware VASE with transparent bluish-green glaze over elaborate moulded decoration. Ht. 40 cm (15.7 in) From a tomb in Hopeh dated late 6th century

and pendant lotus-petals on the upper half of the body; it is covered almost to the bottom of the ovoid body with a yellowish-green glaze.

The shape of this vase and its treatment seems to have led to developments in two directions, one of which lay largely outside the traditional pattern, while the other was to lead on into the T'ang style, with which we are more familiar.

If we take the type that lies outside the traditional pattern first, we find that the earliest example, of A.D. 485, is one of a well-known series of distinctive vases, quite atypical in decoration, which was made intermittently up to the end of the sixth century. A number have come from tombs in Hopei, one being dated to the second half of the sixth century (Plate 57).[5] The type is characterized by the strongly carved or applied relief lotus-petals, in some cases of the cusped type, similar to those found on the pedestals of the contemporary stone sculptures of Buddhist figures.[6] The one in the Nelson Gallery in

5. 'Hopei Ching-hsien Fêng-shih mu', 'The tombs of the Fêng family at Ching-hsien in Hopei' KK 1957, No. 3, pp. 28–37. The latest dated inscription in this group of tombs is A.D. 589.
6. See the pedestal of the Kuan-yin Padmapani from Boston Museum of Fine Arts illustrated in Willetts, *Foundations of Chinese Art*, fig. 133.

58 White stoneware JAR with rouletted and incised decoration under a transparent straw-coloured glaze splashed with green. Ht. 29 cm (11.4 in) Third quarter of 6th century From P'u-yang in Honan

Kansas[7] and that in the Ashmolean Museum in Oxford are probably the most elaborate in the series. The latter (Colour Plate I), lacking the high spreading foot, which has been broken off, is ornamented round the neck with applied reliefs of jewels held between split palmettes and supported by drooping lotus-petals, to which again parallels may be found in Buddhist sculpture.[8] Both the Nelson Gallery and Ashmolean vases are also decorated with jewel motifs in beaded borders which relate to the Central Asian and Fondukistan tradition.[9]

The other more traditional direction to which the decoration of the Hupei vase points stems from the pendant lotus-petals on the upper half of the body. These became a popular feature in the sixth century, were adopted for other shapes and were gradually adapted in a large group of rotund jars, often of noble proportions, many of which have either clay loops on the shoulder or cleanly cut rectangular lugs arranged horizontally or vertically, and either singly or in pairs (Plate 58).[10] In the latter part of the sixth century the high relief of the tips of the petals, which tended to disrupt the bold swelling contours of the vases, was abandoned in favour of an incised line which allowed

7. Illustrated in *STZ* 1956, Vol. 9, Col. Pl. 2.
8. A popular element in late Northern Wei and Ch'i sculpture, the central element often differing. See *Mai-ch'i shan*, Cave 133, stele 11, the lintel above the central Buddha, where the motif occurs five times, each time with a different centre, Pl. 130.
9. J. Auboyer, *The Art of Afghanistan*, London, 1968, Pl. 82 and p. 54 (Musée Guimet MG. 18.860). Freer Gallery lead-glazed vase illustrated in *STZ* 1976, Vol. 11, p. 193, Pl. 168.
10. *The Genius of China*, Exhibition 1973–4, No. 41.

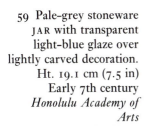

59 Pale-grey stoneware
JAR with transparent
light-blue glaze over
lightly carved decoration.
Ht. 19.1 cm (7.5 in)
Early 7th century
*Honolulu Academy of
Arts*

the eye to travel down the profile without interruption (Plate 59). The clay loops or lugs were retained, and occasionally as in the former Mayer Collection example, the use of a few relief elements occurs (Colour Plate J). In addition to the vases there were also ewers with dragon-headed handles and cock spouts, similarly decorated with carved petals, the profiles of which were low enough not to disturb the line of the body and yet to concentrate interest on the upper part.

By the mid-sixth century the northern stoneware tradition was well established, the body most commonly found being a pale-greyish white or slightly buff colour, variable in density, but always rather hard, and covered with a transparent greenish-yellow, yellow or brown glaze. Some of the greenish glazes, brought about by slight reduction in firing, tend towards blue where they lie thickly on the body. Such jars and ewers as well as deep bowls have been found in Anhui, Honan and Hopei. Other shapes include an early form of the depressed globular vase-shape, which became well known in T'ang times in both earthenware and porcelain. Many of the large jars are well constructed with double clay loops on the shoulder and with the glaze stopping an inch or more short of the base, often being checked either by the tips of the carved petals, or in their absence, by a raised rib a little below the midway line of the body. The unglazed area of the body rarely shows brownish oxidation, a fact which speaks not only of good kiln control, but also suggests that saggars were being used.

In effect by about A.D. 580, the northern kilns were producing quantities of sturdy well-made stonewares suitable for everyday use, in addition to such unusual vases as those in Kansas and Oxford.

Before the end of Sui in A.D. 618, the high-firing of stonewares was everywhere mastered, the bodies being really hard and usually fairly fine grained. Because the quality of the high-fired wares was now so much improved, it may be presumed that they began gradually to replace the lacquer, silver and bronze vessels believed to have been in everyday use in the more wealthy households.

Once the T'ang was firmly established, the economic climate favoured both production and commerce. As a result ceramic development became more rapid. It was from about the end of the second or third decade of the seventh century that specific kilns began to acquire reputations for particular wares, and contemporary and near contemporary authors for the first time refer to some of them. Lu Yü for instance in his *Ch'a-ching*, 'Tea Classic', speaks of the 'yellow-glazed wares of Shou-chou', which almost certainly came from the Yü-chia-k'ou and Ma-chia-kuan kilns just north-east of Shou-chou, and between that city and Huai-nan.[11] These kilns, upon which work has been undertaken in recent years, are of some significance because they cover a period from Northern Ch'i through Sui and into T'ang, from about A.D. 550 until the middle or late seventh century. Not only this, but for the first time among the kiln furnishings saggars were found in addition to spurred stands, and kiln supports.

It was the introduction of saggars and their increasingly widespread use through the sixth century, that led to rapid improvements in stoneware. The practice of packing the wares in saggars is also the key to the production of high-quality ceramics. The protective cases in which the glazed unfired wares are placed ensure not only protection of the glaze from falls of ash in the kiln, such as would scar the fired glaze, but also ensure more even firing-temperatures and conditions through the whole piece, and the results become more consistently good.

The northern wares of the T'ang period can most satisfactorily be treated by dividing them into two groups. Those with coloured glazes, the yellow, yellowish, the wide variety of green, the brownish and the black glazes, making up one very large group, all having almost white, pale-greyish or pale-buff bodies. In the second group are the white-bodied porcellanous wares often slipped and covered with a transparent and virtually colourless glaze. It is best to consider these separately from the stonewares with coloured glazes.

Stonewares with coloured glazes

It is likely in view of sixth-century developments that the transparent yellowish and brownish glazes are earlier than the opaque ones, and most certainly earlier than most of the opaque-brown and the black-glazed wares. Apart from this there is rather meagre information on the coloured stonewares and the dating

11. *WW* 1961, No. 12, pp. 60–6.

60 White stoneware BOWL on tall spreading stem with
impressed and applied decoration under a pale golden-yellow
glaze. Ht. 23 cm (9 in)
From a tomb at Hsi-an dated A.D. 667

remains very uncertain, although there are some shapes which, by analogy with
the lead-glazed earthenwares, can be attributed to the eighth century.

Among the yellowish, almost cream-coloured pieces is the handsomely
proportioned bowl on a high spreading foot, decorated with applied jewel-like
reliefs, which is one of a small number of pieces to be assigned with complete
confidence to the seventh century, as it came from the tomb of Tuan Po-yang
near Ch'ang-an, dated A.D. 667 (Plate 60). The body is dense, almost pure
white, while the glaze has a yellowish-straw tone, which is quite pronounced
where it lies thickly; there is no slip. While the body and glaze colour are by this
time well established, the shape and decoration are unusual, the latter
reflecting the popularity of the Central Asian and Sogdian styles.

The impact of such a decorative treatment is, however, mainly to be found in
the lead-glazed earthenwares and is rarely seen in the common jars, bowls,
dishes and cups. Of these the jars continue to be of the same sturdy
construction found in the sixth century, but the proportions undergo
modification, becoming rounder at the shoulder, while in many cases retaining

61 Buff stoneware EWER
with white slip rouletted
under a brown glaze.
Ht. 14.7 cm (5.8 in)
7th century
*Victoria and Albert
Museum*

the clay loops at the base of the neck. The neck is short and at first wide and straight, but later, in the eighth century, it is found everted at the lip.

Decoration, if it occurs at all, is rather restrained, a feature found equally on the dumpy ewers with a buff body, which has been slipped and rouletted before the application of the brown or yellow glaze (Plate 61). This ewer shape, characterized by the high placement of the short straight spout and the flaring neck was to be standard throughout the T'ang, the body gradually becoming more elongated and ovoid, and the neck longer and less flaring. In the earlier part of the dynasty some of these ewers are believed to have come from the kilns at T'ang-yin in Honan.[12] or from kilns in Shensi. They became more widespread later, especially in Honan, the Yü-hsien kilns having included the shape in their repertory.

The use of slip on the light-coloured bodies in combination with a transparent glaze is found on a very great number of wares in the early part of the dynasty, but bowls, dishes and cups from the Shou-chou kilns in Anhui and Chia-hsien in Honan form a less consistent group.[13] The pale-grey body when left unslipped imparts a distinct brownish tinge to the rather yellow glaze. When the body is slipped the yellow is naturally much cleaner and brighter. The Shou-chou kilns are particularly important because of this variation in treatment, which points to a transition from the pale-yellowish

12. *WW* 1956, No. 7, p. 36; 1957, No. 10, p. 57; 1964, No. 8, p. 1.
13. *WW* 1961, No. 12, pp. 60–6; 1965, No. 9, p. 31.

transparent glazes so common in the sixth century to the more positive brown of the seventh century, a good fragmentary example of which was found in the excavation.[14] The dark-brown-glazed vase of fairly large size in Plate 62 is similar to the excavated example, while the Chicago one is handsomely proportioned with a cupped mouth and horizontally ribbed neck that looks forward to the amphora shape so common in the lead-glazed wares of the late seventh and early eighth century (Plate 63). Like the fragmentary vase from Shou-chou it is decorated round the shoulder with applied reliefs, reminiscent of the Ashmolean vase but used with a greater restraint, suggesting a dying fashion.

From the late seventh century onward, the dark-brown opaque glazes and

14. *WW* 1961, No. 12, p. 61.

62 Grey stoneware V A S E with brown glaze, the unglazed part of the exposed body oxidized red. Dimensions not known 6th–7th century Excavated from a tomb in Shantung

63 Pale-grey stoneware V A S E with pale-greenish glaze. Ht. 41.5 cm (16.3 in) 7th century *Chicago Art Institute*

the black glazes become more frequent, and excavations indicate that black wares were made at most of the more important centres to which a T'ang date can be assigned. Fragments have been found in quantity at Ho-pi-chi, Chia-hsien and Kung-hsien in Honan all of which would appear to have operated from the late seventh or early eighth century, and later the groups of kilns around Yü-hsien in Honan[15] and Yao-chou in Shensi[16] contributed their share, making brown and yellowish-glazed wares as well.

The earlier black and brown wares, continuing up to about the middle of the eighth century, include a number of examples of ewers with well-rounded bodies, similar in shape to some of the forms in the lead-glazed wares (Colour Plate K). The ewer with rather elaborate handle in the British Museum is a good example of the type (Plate 64). It shows the quality of the glaze in its full application to the body, its good fit, and its excellent control. The smooth matt surface is an indication of very slow cooling, which is fairly characteristic of the early black wares as well as of much of the opaque-glazed material (Plate 65). Where these rather splendid pieces were made is not known, but the province of Honan may be suggested as so much dark-glazed pottery has been found in excavations here, one of the most important kiln sites being that at Chia-hsien.

In Huang-t'ao, not far from Chia-hsien county town, the probable ancestor of Chün was found.[17] This again is a kiln where slow cooling of the fired wares seems to have been normal. It is thus possible that many vessels, jars, spherical ewers with narrow necks, and vases, some of gourd shape with or without loop handles, dishes and alms-bowls, with either a dark-brown or black glaze suffused with grey-blue, came from these kilns (Colour Plates L and M, Plate 66). There are also examples with a pale, opaque grey glaze with dark suffusions. All have a relatively fine-grained pale-buff body which is very hard, with the glaze applied by dipping, often not reaching the base, and lying in the swag-like curves that are characteristic of this method of glaze application. In most instances the foot is slightly spread, bevelled at the edge and flat across the base. They are nearly always neatly finished.

Green-glazed, celadon-type wares until recently have hardly appeared at all in north China during this period so the find in a tomb near Ch'ang-an dating to A.D. 665 of a bowl of this type is something of an exception and may well be an import. It seems to have a fairly thick body, although it is well made and neatly finished. It is four lobed and completely covered with glaze, apparently being fired on a three-spurred support on the foot-ring, so that small scars remain. At present there is no indication as to where it was made. Some examples are identified by Tregear in the Ingram Collection in the Ashmolean Museum.[18] They somewhat resemble the one early specimen in technique of firing on stands that leave spur-marks on the foot-ring, and although there are

15. WW 1964, No. 8, p. 27 et seq.
16. Shensi Tung-ch'üan Yao-chou yao, Peking, 1965, p. 7.
17. WW 1951, No. 2, p. 53.
18. M. Tregear, Catalogue of Chinese Greenwares, Nos. 239 and 241.

64 Grey stoneware EWER
with a dense black glaze.
Ht. 27.6 cm (10.8 in)
8th century
British Museum

65 Stoneware EWER
with a smooth, matt,
dense brownish-black
glaze.
Ht. 24.1 cm (9.5 in)
8th–9th century
*Asian Art Museum of
San Francisco*

66 Stoneware DISH with bluish phosphatic splashing on a dense brownish-black
glaze. Diameter 25.1 cm (9.9 in)
9th century
British Museum

one or two pieces that slightly resemble it in shape, others are quite different
being rounder in contour.

White wares

It is clear from the tomb finds alone that the potters of north China had already
achieved a white-bodied porcellanous ware even before the beginning of the
T'ang. In the tomb of Chang Shêng, dated A.D. 595,[19] a considerable number
of white pieces were found, some of them of rather unusual shapes, such as an
incense-burner of *po-shan-lu* type in a tray, and a curious object resembling a
candelabra. There were also some handsome storage-jars and a vase with
applied reliefs, a number of simpler bowls and a small covered jar of elegant

19. *KK* 1959, No. 10, p. 541 et seq.

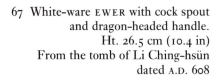

67 White-ware EWER with cock spout and dragon-headed handle.
Ht. 26.5 cm (10.4 in)
From the tomb of Li Ching-hsün
dated A.D. 608

waisted shape. The next example was the bird-spouted ewer with a dragon-headed handle from the richly furnished tomb of Li Ching-hsün, dated A.D. 608 (Plate 67).[20] This object has a white glaze over a fine-grained whitish body. The other vessels in the tomb were all of whitish stoneware but with transparent greenish glaze. Finally there was a double-bodied amphora and a white-glazed pilgrim-bottle of which the example in Toronto is a duplicate from the same mould.[21]

It seems fair to assume that all the pieces from these two tombs were of northern manufacture. They are not porcelain in the accepted European sense, in as much as they appear from the illustrations, and from the descriptions in the Chinese texts, to be fairly thick and heavy and thus unlikely to be translucent.

The development of the northern white wares during the first century of the T'ang dynasty is still uncertain, but it is possible to include in the seventh century such white jars as the one in the British Museum (Plate 68). But this is

20. *KK* 1959, No. 9, p. 471 et seq. See also *STZ* 1976, Vol. 11, pp. 194, 170.
21. *Unearthing China's Past*, Boston, 1973, figs. 79 and 80.

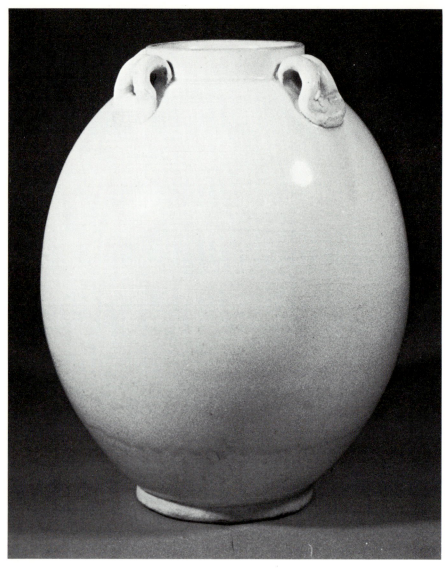

68   White-ware JAR with loops on shoulder. Ht. 30.5 cm (12 in)
Late 7th century
British Museum

certainly a stoneware, lacking the pure whiteness of body that became a feature
of the porcellanous wares which were to increase later. However, by the early
eighth century there is evidence from tomb finds that among the smaller and
simpler shapes there was a repertory common to the earthenwares, stonewares
and porcellanous wares. The well-known depressed globular vase with cupped
mouth, for instance, is found through the whole range (Plate 69); so too is the
admirably simple-shaped cup (Plate 70) and the small cup with ring handle,
but the elegant stem-cup is found only in the porcellanous ware (Plate 71).

69 Depressed globular white-ware JAR AND COVER.
Ht. 10.8 cm (4.2 in)
8th century
Boston Museum of Fine Arts

70 White-ware CUP. Ht. 9.2 cm (3.6 in)
7th–8th century
British Museum

71 Porcellanous STEM-CUP.
Ht. 7.9 cm (3.1 in)
7th–8th century
Victoria and Albert Museum

72 Porcellanous BOWL. Diameter 10.5 cm (4.1 in)
    8th century
    Carl Kempe Collection

Among the bowl shapes that may safely be attributed to the eighth century are
those with a clearly defined metal ancestry as represented by one in the Kempe
Collection (Plate 72).

Until the late eighth century it is almost impossible to know where these
white wares were made, as so far the excavated kiln sites seem only to have
yielded evidence of activity from the middle or late T'ang times onward. On
the present evidence the foremost centres were in Honan and Hopei, with the
greatest number of sites, seven, recorded in Honan, where Ho-pi-chi, Chia-
hsien, Mi-hsien, Têng-fêng Hsien and Kung-hsien are among the most
important. In Hopei, Chü-yang, later to become famous for Ting ware, is so far
the only kiln complex known to have been producing top quality porcellanous
wares, a foreshadowing of the later achievements of the Sung dynasty.

Ho-pi-chi's main production of white ware seems to have been of bowls,
most of which were wide mouthed and low, with wide-spreading almost
straight sides, thickened at the rim and with a low, sometimes wide foot-ring, a
classic shape in late T'ang white ware. Most were not of the highest quality, as
the bowls usually have three spur-marks on the glaze inside, indicating that
they were stacked for firing. Ewers had the next most important place, and
these were of the short-spouted type (Plate 73), often with lugs on the
shoulder, a rather wide tall neck, and a strap handle which usually carried
impressed decoration. Most later ewers were fairly tall (Plate 74) and much less
rotund than the ones found in the buff stoneware with yellow or brown glaze
described earlier. They were generally covered with a white slip in order to
conceal the imperfections of the dirty white body. The use of slip under the

73 White-ware EWER.
Ht. 25.4 cm (10 in)
8th century
Honolulu Academy of Arts

74 White stoneware EWER slipped
and transparently glazed.
Ht. 15.3 cm (6 in)
9th century
Victoria and Albert Museum

transparent colourless glaze of course enhanced the impression of whiteness. The glaze itself is certainly alkaline, that is free of lead, but may not have been feldspathic. Many specimens seem to have had a dash of green from copper fritted with lead as decoration.

Among the other kilns making these ewers were Mi-hsien and Têng-fêng, the latter also making foliated bowls with a small neat foot-ring instead of a low wide one.[22] These two kilns came into operation in T'ang, Mi-hsien perhaps in the late eighth century, and Têng-Fêng probably in the ninth. Mi-hsien ceased production early in Sung but Têng-fêng continued into the late eleventh century or even later. Neither kiln made a porcellanous ware, the products being a pale greyish-white or buff stoneware, invariably slipped before the application of the colourless glaze.

Inevitably the question of Hsing-chou and the fabled Hsing ware must be discussed, but there is little here to detain us long. Lu Yü's oft-quoted comment that Hsing bowls resembled silver is well known.[23] Unfortunately, although the location of Hsing-chou is known, as well as the village in that prefecture in Hopei where it is traditionally believed to have been made, no kiln evidence of any kind has yet been discovered. Moreover even if there were kilns, which is now very questionable, it seems unlikely that they will ever be found. This is because of the repeated flooding of the region down the centuries by the Yellow River, which has also changed its course on several occasions since the T'ang dynasty. It has to be borne in mind also, that a market centre may have given its name to a ware made elsewhere, and this seems the more likely explanation in view of recent archaeological work carried out by the Chinese. As the result of such work we know of one group of kilns already active in the T'ang dynasty making high-quality porcellanous ware. This is the group in Ting-chou prefecture in the province of Hopei, the kilns themselves being located sixteen miles north of Chü-yang and about thirty-five miles north-west of modern Ting-hsien.

The kilns achieved the zenith of their fame in the Northern Sung and Chin periods, but were already in production early in the ninth century, or perhaps even earlier. They were discovered by Fujio Koyama in 1941 and briefly reported at that time in Japan, but not until 1948 in a European language.[24] Ch'ên Wan-li visited and briefly surveyed the site in 1952, and subsequently Fêng Hsien-ming made an exploratory survey in 1958, upon which he published a short report. Further and more extensive work was undertaken in 1961–2 and the illustrated report, still relatively brief, was published in 1965.[25] It is clear from the accumulation of reports that the kilns were making excellent

22. *WW* 1964, No. 3, pp. 47–55, and foot of p. 45.
23. *Ch'a-ching*, 'Classic of Tea', supposed to have been composed in the eighth century.
24. J. M. Plumer, 'The Ting-yao kiln sites: Koyama's significant discoveries', *Archives of the Chinese Art Society of America*, 3, 1948–9, pp. 61–6.
25. *KK* 1965, No. 8, pp. 394–412; a summary translation in Oriental Ceramic Society, *Chinese Translations*, No. 4.

J   Pale-greyish stoneware JAR AND LID with relief decoration. Ht. 34cm (13.4in)
Late 6th century
Formerly Mr. F. M. Mayer Collection. See page 67

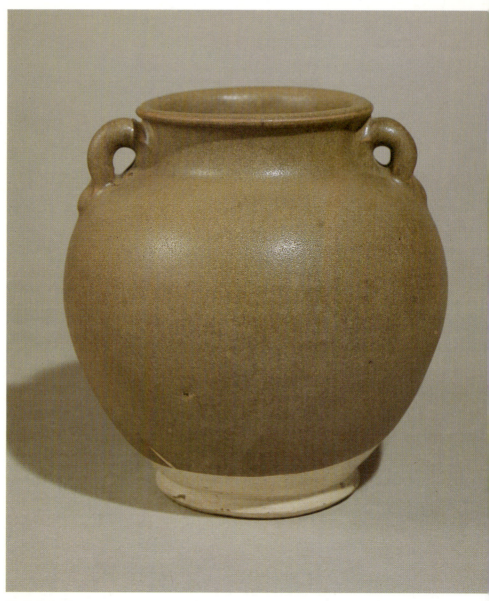

K Pale-buff stoneware JAR with speckled brown glaze; flat base. Ht. 12.5cm (4.9in)
7th–8th century
Percival David Foundation. See page 72

75 White porcelain CUP-STAND. Diameter 9.5 cm (3.7 in)
8th–9th century
Carl Kempe Collection

76 White porcelain BOWL with thickened rim. Diameter 13.3 cm (5.2 in)
9th century
Formerly Toller Collection

ware by the ninth century, but at present there is little indication of how much before that date the operations were begun. As the result of all the work so far carried out, Fêng Hsien-ming commented in 1965 that the tradition associated with Hsing-chou would have to be reconsidered, in the light of the finds made at the Ting kilns, which suggest a prior claim in importance.

It was during the T'ang that tea-drinking became popular, and this did much to stimulate invention and undoubtedly accounts for the appearance of cup-stands (Plate 75). These are known in silver and silver gilt and make their appearance in the eighth century. They also occur in the porcellanous wares of the Ting kilns in the course of perhaps the late eighth century, but certainly in the ninth century.

As the result of the excavations of the Ting kilns we now have a fairly clear picture of the ninth-century repertory of shapes, and it is possible to parallel many of the pieces in collections elsewhere with the finds, chief among which are the so-called Samarra-type bowls with the low wide foot-ring and thickened rim, which previously had been conjecturally attributed to Hsing (Plates 76, 77a and b). Foliated and lobed bowls were to continue through the tenth century and these too were found in the Ting kiln-sites. Deep well-rounded bowls with either a thickened rim (Plate 78) or with a tastefully worked pastry-band at the rim (Plate 79) can now be traced back with confidence to the Ting kilns.

Among the vertical shapes two types of ewer can be identified, one of which has already been encountered in the stonewares from Têng-fêng.[26] This is the ewer with ovoid body and tall spreading neck, but now this has become more trumpet-like at the lip (Plate 80). The spout remains short and set high on the shoulder. The loop handle may be simple, or may be elaborated with an extra band or a curl of clay near the top. The base is generally slightly spread and flat, although there are some examples which have a low square-cut foot-ring. The other type of ewer is similar in shape as regards the body but the neck is shorter, less flared to the lip, and the handle is in the form of a lion, with hind legs on the shoulder, the body bending up and round in a loop to grip the lip of the vessel in its jaws (Plate 81). These usually seem to have a flat base and like the first type it spreads a little.

Particularly numerous among the white porcellanous wares are round boxes, sometimes with high-domed lid, sometimes with a flat one. They are always very well made and have the neat square-cut foot-ring also found on some of the ewers.

The body material is very like that of the subsequent Sung period Ting material, being dense, fine-grained and pure white. Despite the natural whiteness and the porcellanous character of the body, it was generally slipped before the application of the transparent glaze during the T'ang period, and possibly for some decades into the tenth century. Bowls were very often slipped

26. See note 22 above.

77a White porcelain BOWL of Samarra type. Diameter 14.4 cm (5.6 in)
9th century
Percival David Foundation

77b Base of white Samarra-type porcelain BOWL. Diameter 14.4 cm (5.6 in)
9th century
Percival David Foundation

78 White porcellanous BOWL. Diameter 10.1 cm (3.9 in)
    9th–10th century
    Ashmolean Museum

79 White porcelain BOWL with pastry-work rim. White slip under the colourless
    glaze. Diameter 12.4 cm (4.9 in)
    9th century
    Formerly Lord Cunliffe Collection

80 White porcelain EWER with white-slipped body. Ht. 14.5 cm (5.7 in)
9th century
Victoria and Albert Museum

only on the inside, and the indication that they are slipped can usually be
determined by a tendency of the slip to spill over from the inside onto the
outside and run down a little in a kind of tear-mark under the glaze. In the
firing the glaze sometimes acquires a cold bluish, or more rarely greenish, tone
where it lies thickly. Sometimes we find examples of a warm ivory colour, but
these are not very numerous. Such differences in colour are due to the
fortuitous reduction or oxidation in the firing, the bluish and greenish tones
being the result of reduction, and the ivory of oxidation.

81 White porcellanous
EWER with lion
handle. Ht. 12.2 cm
(4.8 in)
8th–9th century
Ashmolean Museum

82 White porcelain JAR.
Ht. 10.5 cm (4.1 in)
Ashmolean Museum

The ware is in every case very well fired and whatever the tone of the glaze it generally has a high gloss. In some cases the pieces may be translucent. Whether the translucency is due solely to the firing temperature and the natural character of the materials, or is due to additions of dolomite, as seems to have been the case in Sung times, is not at present known.[27] The problems relating to body and glaze type can only be resolved by Chinese analysis of sherds of known T'ang date which have come from the site.

The most important feature of these early white porcellanous wares from north China is the almost total absence of decoration (Plate 82). Not only this, but most of the specimens are small, not often exceeding about twenty centimetres (eight inches) in diameter or height, and with few exceptions of very simple form. This may well be due to the character of the material, which was probably not very plastic. The lack of plasticity would make it very difficult to throw large pieces, and in any case there must have been a good deal of handwork involved in shaving the walls of vessels to the required thinness. The developments of the tenth century are those which one would expect, in as much as we find an increasing refinement in the control of the firing, as well as a refining of the shapes and greater thinness of the walls of vessels being sought.

While the shapes in the coloured stonewares of the period are frequently held in common with those current in the lead-glazed earthenwares, there are many fewer shapes common to the white wares. Shapes in the coloured stonewares are even more rarely found in common with those of the porcellanous wares. For instance the globular ewer with short narrow neck and everted mouth, so common in lead-glazed wares and stonewares (Colour Plate M), does not occur at all in the porcellanous wares, but the taller ovoid type with a longer neck is of quite frequent occurrence (Plate 74). It is just possible that a factor relating to chronology may be involved here, but more evidence is needed. The bowl shapes, which in most wares are simple, are occasionally complicated in the porcellanous wares by a pastry-worked frilly rim, something entirely absent from the other wares. Again there may be a chronological factor involved, but in this case the difference could be accounted for by the materials used. The answers to problems such as these can only be satisfactorily found as the result of further excavation and finds of more closely datable material.

27. N. Sundius, 'Some aspects of the technical development in the manufacture of Chinese pottery wares of the pre-Ming age', *Bulletin of the Museum of Far Eastern Antiquities*, Stockholm, 33, 1961, pp. 103–24.

Chapter 5
SOUTHERN WARES

During the T'ang period the sites of pottery manufacture in the south seem to have been as widely dispersed as they were varied in character, including as they do earthenwares and stonewares. Of the southern centres the best known is probably Ch'ang-sha in Hunan although in fact the kilns themselves lie well to the north of the city. In the other southern provinces groups of kilns are found in the vicinity of Lo-p'ing and Nan-fêng, as well as Fou-liang Hsien in Kiangsi, and in Szechwan there are a few kilns to the north of Ch'êng-tu. Activity in T'ang times has been reported at kilns in Fukien, Kuangsi and in the vicinity of Canton in Kuang-tung, but little has been published so far about their production at this time. The most common products of all these centres, with the possible exception of those in Szechwan, were imitations of the northern Chekiang celadons of Yüeh type, and a variety of white or near-white wares. The study of the wares from these different centres is in its infancy, not least because although sites have been located and surveyed, relatively little excavation has taken place, and even less has been published.

Hunan

The only group of sites to have been comparatively well investigated are those in the large central province of Hunan. Traditionally Yo-chou, at the north-east corner of the Tung-t'ing lake, a centre mentioned by Lu Yü in his *Ch'a-ching*, 'Tea Classic', was the one regarded as most important, but the name of Ch'ang-sha, to the south of the lake, has also long been associated with ceramics. In the T'ang period this more southerly area would appear gradually to have superseded Yo-chou.[1] Tomb finds in the neighbourhood of the city, and in the country to the north towards the lake have yielded considerable quantities of pottery of various kinds which first appeared on the market in the late 1940s. These suggested that there must have been a long period of activity and large production in the area. Dr. Isaac Newton, in a series of papers from

1. The name is sometimes transcribed Yüeh-chou, which was the name in T'ang and Sung times. The name was changed to the now more familiar Yo-chou in 1899.

1950 onward drew attention to the wares and in two of these papers he attempted a preliminary classification of them.[2]

Newton made it clear that there was a wide variety of both bodies and glazes in the area, and that activity at the kilns producing the wares extended over a long period. We are not here concerned with the large body of pre-T'ang material, but only with that from about the seventh century onward. Not unnaturally certain revisions are necessary to Newton's classification and also to his dating, particularly as the result of work undertaken by the Chinese in the late 1950s, most of it published in 1960. Until the Chinese reports were published it was generally believed that Yo-chou was the main centre of production, but in fact the most advanced and prolific group of kilns was at T'ung-kuan, a little south of the Tung-t'ing lake, between Yo-chou and Ch'ang-sha.[3]

Earthenware, stoneware and porcelain are recorded, but the porcelain is not well enough published to justify discussion here. Common to all sites in Hunan, as to those in other provinces, were greenwares. Some were identified in the local variant from the Yo-chou district as having come from the T'ieh-kuan-chieh kiln site, discovered in 1953, but others to which we refer below, came from Wa-ch'a-p'ing. The shapes from T'ieh-kuan-chieh kiln included bowls, dishes, jars and ewers of typical late T'ang type, some with minimal decoration. The decoration was simple consisting of incised lines and rings, with occasional instances of moulding in the centre of a bowl.

Jars and ewers tend to be a little more stocky and rounder than the Yüeh ones. The body is often slipped and the glaze is very thin and glassy. It is an alkaline glaze, rather high in calcium and so has a strong tendency to craze and peel off. The bowls thought to be the earliest, are flat across the base with only a slight flare to the foot; later the foot-ring was cut and the base left unglazed. In fact the glaze rarely reached the bottom. It was quite common at all times to stack the bowls on four or five spurs for the firing. Sometimes the scars left after firing are large and untidy, and at other times they are small and neat. The jars from Yo-chou may be ornamented with large dark-brown splashes on the shoulder around the lugs so frequently placed at the junction of the neck and shoulder (Plate 83). These lugs may be set either vertically or horizontally. The bodies of all apparently late T'ang Yo-chou wares are usually greyish, and the slip where this occurs, is a paler grey and not really white. Among the mass of materials of so-called Yo-chou origin found in the vicinity of Ch'ang-sha were others, painted in green, sometimes turquoise, and brown with either a white, or a yellowish or greenish glaze, which do not match any of the finds from T'ieh-kuan-chieh, so there had to be another kiln site.

2. I. Newton, 'A thousand years of potting in Hunan Province', *TOCS* 26, 1950–1, pp. 27–36 and *FECB*, No. 40, 1958, pp. 3–50.
3. The most valuable article in Chinese is Fêng Hsien-ming's in *WW* 1960, No. 3, pp. 71–4, which summarizes all the work previously undertaken and published piecemeal in *KK* from 1953 onwards. There is also a useful report on Wa-ch'a-p'ing in the same number, pp. 67–70.

83 Yo-chou type JAR with dark-brown
    splashes on the shoulder and square-
    cut lugs. Ht. 13.6 cm (5.3 in)
    Ashmolean Museum

84 Imitation of Yüeh VASE from
    Ch'ang-sha with the greenish
    glaze breaking up. The dark line
    two-thirds of the way down the
    body shows the limit of the two-
    layered glaze. Dimensions not
    known
    9th century

In 1956 the new and very important kilns near T'ung-kuan were found at
Wa-ch'a-p'ing. The sites are on the east bank of the Hsiang river, a little over
twenty miles north of Ch'ang-sha. Numerous old clay-pits and refuse heaps
were found as well as a number of very dilapidated ruins of kilns. The kilns
produced both earthenwares and stonewares, and included the popular green-
glazed wares in both types of body, the stoneware type being conscious
imitations of Yüeh (Plate 84), but easily distinguished from it on account of the
sometimes indifferent adhesion of the alkaline glaze, and the slightly less dense
and hard body. There is in fact considerable variation in the fineness and
hardness of the bodies from the different kilns in the area, but generally the
colour of glaze and the decorations remain fairly uniform.

The imitations of Yüeh ware are seen best in the bowls, which are generally
of two types. Either the foot is slightly spread and flat across the base, the glaze
stopping just short of the foot, or they have a small foot-ring, are glazed all over
and are fired on a five-spurred stand. The latter type is probably later and the
quality is a good deal better than that of the flat-based type. Those with a flat
base have simple rounded sides and sometimes flare to a straight rim or are

85 Yüeh-type BOWL AND COVER from Ch'ang-sha.
    Diameter 14.6 cm (5.7 in)
    9th century
    Seattle Art Museum

86 Base and cover of Yüeh-type BOWL (Plate 85)
    Seattle Art Museum

everted to a four-lobed rim, in some cases with arc-shaped segments cut from
each lobe. The glaze is a single thin application tending to craze and peel off.

The bowls with a foot-ring have a fine pale-greyish body, and the walls are
relatively thin and the shapes simple. These are among the closest imitations of
Yüeh but are unusual because the glaze may be applied in two layers. The
Seattle bowl and cover is an admirable example of the type (Plates 85 and 86).
The glaze surface has a high gloss and a slightly watery appearance, and

87 Base of Yüeh-type
BOWL showing single
layer of glaze on base,
foot-ring and lower
part of body. Diameter
16.8 cm (6.6 in)
*Percival David
Foundation Study
Collection*

although the glaze is crazed it seems to have quite good adhesion. This type probably continued well into the Five Dynasties period and seems to have been popular. Many pieces, especially bowls, were fired on spurred stands instead of on the foot-ring, five spurs being the most common (Plate 87).

The kilns of Wa-ch'a-p'ing are of particular importance because it was here that the decorated stonewares and polychrome-painted earthenwares were produced. Perhaps the best-known products of the kilns were the sturdy greyish stoneware ewers with moulded reliefs on the sides under dark-brown patches in the yellowish or greenish glaze. The ewers have a flat unglazed base and a slightly spread, neatly cut low foot. On the rounded shoulder is usually a short hexagonal or octagonal spout, two ribbed lugs at the sides, and a strap handle (Plate 88). The neck, which is clearly articulated, spreads to a straight sometimes thickened lip. The thin glaze is applied very evenly and stops about half an inch short of the base. Ewers of this type have been found in Korea as well as in many other parts of China, but they are probably best known from the sherd material on Islamic sites such as Nishapur in the northern province of Khurasan in Iran, and at Siraf on the Persian Gulf, as well as on innumerable sites in Indonesia. An interesting feature of some of the ewers is that inscriptions in brown are sometimes found on them. These read *Ch'ia-chia Hsiao-k'ou t'ien-hsia yu-ming*, 'Ch'ia family wares are world famous', or *Chêng-chia hsiao-k'ou t'ien-hsia ti-i*, 'Chêng family wares are first in the world', and the name of Chang is also known with similar wording.

The jars to be identified with this group of sites are of somewhat similar sturdy form, but with a wide straight mouth often thickened at the rim (Plate 89). Some were on the kiln site, but others have been found in tombs in the locality. There is usually a pair of small lugs on the shoulder, and like the ewers they have a flat base. One found in a tomb in the vicinity is of special

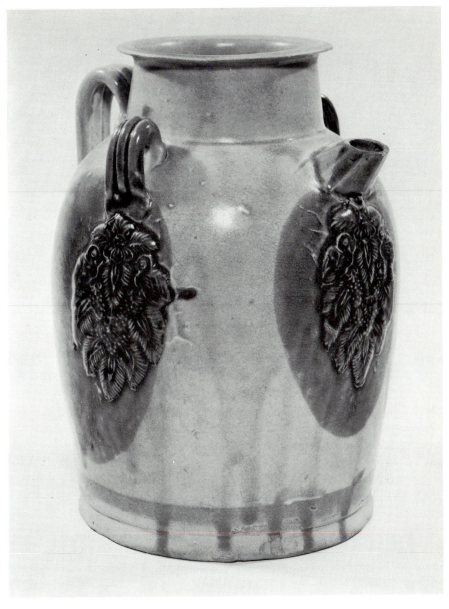

88 T'ung-kuan, Wa-ch'a-p'ing type, stoneware EWER with applied reliefs on a
pale-greyish slip with brown glaze. Ht. 22.5 cm (8.8 in)
8th–9th century
Cleveland Museum of Art

89 Stoneware JAR with
brown and green spots in
the pale-buff glaze.
Ht. 14.5 cm (5.7 in)
9th century
Japanese collection

importance because it had green painting in a white glaze. Other jars from the kiln site have been found with green or brown painting on them, usually in spotted designs. Probably one of the finest examples is that recently found at Yang-chou in Anhui, reported in 1978 and dated mid-T'ang.[4] According to Fêng Hsien-ming the pieces with spotted decoration of this kind on both jars and ewers could not be dated earlier than T'ang, and he implies that the style continued into the Five Dynasties.

Only slightly less familiar than the ewers and jars are the bowls with similar greyish body painted in brown and green, or in brown alone under an almost colourless or yellowish transparent glaze; they usually have freely scribbled designs (Plate 90). The firing is well controlled and the decoration clearly defined. These pieces are rarely more than about twenty centimetres (eight inches) in diameter, and rather shallow, with slightly rounded walls straight at the rim. The painted green colour on some pieces may appear bluish, so that the suggestion has been made that cobalt blue was used. This is not the case, however, as the green is derived from copper oxide combined in a frit with a small quantity of lead. Where the bluish tone occurs, this is due to a rather low lead content or an excessive amount of copper, which leaks into the alkaline glaze and is thus turned to a turquoise tone. Bowls of this type have now been found, like the ewers, in the Near East at both Nishapur and Siraf.[5]

4. *WW* 1978, No. 3, Pl. 1 in colour. See also p. 80.
5. C. K. Wilkinson, *Nishapur: Pottery of the Early Islamic Period*, 1974, p. 257, No. 13; also D. Whitehouse, 'Excavations at Siraf; fourth interim report', *Iran*, 9, 1971, Pls. VIIIa and c.

90 BOWLS painted in green and brown, excavated at Nishapur.
   Diameter *left* 13.8 cm (5.4 in), *right* 14 cm (5.5 in)
   left: *Professor T. Mikami Collection.* right: *Japanese collection*

Other shapes decorated in this way include head-rests (Plate 91), some of them painted on the top surface with beautiful sprays of flowers and with birds. There are also designs which, according to Fêng Hsien-ming, have the contours finely incised and then have the colours applied within the contours before the application of the glaze.

Differing in some ways from these, but also made at Wa-ch'a-p'ing are lobed or foliated bowls (Plate 92), some of an almost closed flower form, and head-

91 Stoneware HEAD-REST painted in green and brown, with
   some incising and an olive glaze. Length 17 cm (6.7 in)
   8th–9th century
   Boston Museum of Fine Arts

rests, painted in an opaque white alkaline glaze with copper green and in a few cases with iron brown. The decorations are for the most part simply grouped dots or small comma-like strokes of the brush, the latter being organized into some sort of design. Again the glaze crazes and seems rather soft, but it does not appear to peel off easily as some of the transparent ones do.

Characteristic of these wares broadly identified with Ch'ang-sha is the reddish discolouration of the surface of many pieces, and the crazing of the glaze. The colour is due to the red soil in which so much of the material has been buried down the centuries.

A certain number of sherds have been picked up on the T'ung-kuan sites which have come from moulded bowls with moulded decoration inside and also from some small boxes with moulded lids, but although we are told that some of these are green-glazed earthenware, there is insufficient published evidence at present to make positive identifications possible. Nevertheless, the small square dishes like that illustrated (Colour Plate N) may well be examples of this group.[6]

Of particular interest to the ceramic historian is the simultaneous appearance in these Ch'ang-sha wares of lead and leadless glazes, transparent and opaque alkaline glazes, the use of fritted copper and lead oxide to produce a stable green in a leadless glaze, and the introduction of underglaze painting. It is likely to be a puzzle for some time to come as to why polychrome decoration of this kind having been discovered, it did not spread to other kilns. It seems that the T'ung-kuan kilns barely survived the Five Dynasties period, for nothing is recorded of them in the Sung period.

Kiangsi

It is slightly surprising in view of the fame of Ching-tê Chên in later centuries that so little is known of the earlier periods of production, that is before the Sung dynasty. Indeed very few kiln sites of T'ang date have so far been identified and studied, even in the province of Kiangsi as a whole.

In Fou-liang Hsien, the county in which the great kiln complex of Ching-tê Chên is situated, Yang-mei-t'ing about two miles from Hu-t'ien, Hsiang-hu about eight miles north-east of Ching-tê Chên, and Shih-hu-wan all produced quite good green-glazed wares in imitation of Yüeh tradition. At Yang-mei-t'ing,[7] the best-studied group, the bowls were very simple with rounded sides and straight rim, and the bases were flat. There were marks of firing-stands both inside and outside on the bottom so that they were evidently stacked inside rather tall saggars, of which fragments were also found. One of the few examples of ewers from this site so far published, strongly resembles the Yüeh type.

6. D. Whitehouse, 'Excavations at Siraf: fifth interim report', Pl. XI, which seems to be another example in the same series, and may also come from a Ch'ang-sha kiln. Both specimens share the common feature of a chevron pattern at the angles in the walls inside.
7. *WW* 1955, No. 8, p. 111 et seq.

L   Pale-buff stoneware JAR of Huang-tʻao type. Ht. 39.5cm (15.5in)
7th–8th century
Newark Museum. See page 72

M Stoneware EWER of Huang-t'ao type. Ht. 14.5cm (5.7in)
8th century
Museen für Ostasiatische Kunst, Staatliche Museen Preussischer Kulturbesitz, Berlin.
See pages 72 and 87

92 T'ung-kuan CUP and small DISH painted in dull turquoise-green on an opaque
white glaze. Diameter of cup 9.5 cm (3.7 in), and dish 14 cm (5.5 in)
9th century
Victoria and Albert Museum

To the south of these two sites, between twenty-five and thirty miles away, a
short distance from Lo-p'ing, is Nan-yao ts'un.[8] Here there were considerable
resources of whitish clay and a clay-pit was found from which the kilns were
supplied. The products again included simple bowls, but here there was a
properly cut foot with a slight recess in the centre. The glaze, uneven and
crazed was greenish brown. Some of the larger, deeper bowls had a groove cut
round the outside just below the rim, and some were brown glazed. Small
dishes of between twelve and fifteen centimetres (four and a half and six inches)
in diameter had a red burnt or greyish-brown body, the former with a
yellowish-brown oxidized glaze and the latter with a greenish-brown
reduction-fired glaze. These again were stacked up on firing-stands in the
saggars so that they have scars inside and outside. In addition to these pieces
there were some heavily constructed, rather coarse-bodied jars and vases with
'drum-shaped' bodies with long necks, both shapes with a blackish-brown
glaze.

Much farther to the south at Lin-ch'üan near Fu-chou, south of the P'o-
yang lake, a group of three kilns at Pai-ch'üan-yao was found and among the
finds was some T'ang material.[9] The bowls were of similar shape to those of
Yang-mei-t'ing in the north, but had a small recess in the base. They were
covered with a watery uneven glaze and were much crazed. Again the pieces
were fired in stacks on stands. The body material of these bowls was rather

8. *KK* 1966, No. 5, pp. 260–2.
9. *KK* 1963, No. 12, p. 686 et seq.

thick, heavy and coarse. There was a group of flat-based bowls and some of these had small floral decorations inside, but we are not told how the decoration was executed. This type had a thin fine-grained grey body. Other material included flat-bottomed sturdy jars with brownish or black glazes reaching to just below the mid-body line; the exposed body was rather coarse and grey. Large jars of *kuan* type also had a flat base, but had lugs on the shoulder and small applied-relief heads. They were similarly coarse bodied, but were fully glazed inside and outside.

The material from the sites was very similar to what had already been found in Nan-Chao and Sui tombs in the vicinity, so it was suggested that this group of kilns was active at a relatively early date and continued production into the early part of the T'ang period. It is clear from this summary that work has scarcely begun.

Szechwan

Pottery production in west China is little known and the number of sites so far identified, studied and reported in the literature is very small. Those that are known and on which brief reports have been published all lie in the region of Ch'eng-tu, and of these the Ch'ing-yang-kung site appears to be the most important, followed by the Shih-fang-t'ang kiln in Ch'iung-lai Hsien, and Mo-ma Shan. These were all producing in T'ang times, the Ch'ing-yang-kung kiln continuing through the Five Dynasties into the Sung period.

The paucity of published materials makes it difficult, if not impossible to identify wares from these sites at present and it is only possible to describe what they were making in very general terms.

The Ch'ing-yang-kung site is well defined and was fairly rich in finds, the bulk of the material being a heavy hard earthenware.[10] The bodies are fine grained and most pieces fired to a reddish tone, but there was also a small amount of grey as well as white-bodied material. The glazes used are described as being brown or *ch'ing-pai*,[11] the vessels being glazed most of the way down the outside. There was also a celadon type, but this was rare. The decoration includes underglaze painting in reddish-brown and green with a white glaze (Plate 93); this type has parallels with Wa-ch'a-p'ing. On the brown-glazed pieces only there was impressed decoration, and on these there was also applied relief.

The white glaze, usually with a greenish shade, is reputed to be rather thin and watery with a tendency to craze. It was normally only found on the smaller pieces like cups, small bowls and dishes. The larger dishes are said usually to be white inside and brown outside.

10. *WW* 1956, No. 6, p. 53 et seq.
11. *Ch'ing-pai* is a general term meaning white with a faint bluish or greenish tinge in the reports on ceramics; it is very widely applied to white wares, not being confined to the Ch'ing-tê Chên type.

93 Stoneware JAR partly slipped and painted in brown and green on a
    white glaze. Ht. 17.3 cm (6.8 in)
    9th–10th century
    Present whereabouts not known

The much larger pieces such as big dishes and jars were brown glazed, the
glaze varying in both thickness and colour; it did not reach the base. When thin
it is described as being 'tea yellow', a nice descriptive term but not very helpful.

The vessels are all reported to be wheel-made. In the firing the wares were
stacked, and although much kiln furniture was found that included suitable
spurred stands and ring supports, there is no mention of saggars, but it seems
likely that in fact they were used.

Shih-fang-t'ang site is also quite important, and is unusual in as much as
sufficient remained of the kiln to indicate that it was similar, but not identical to
the later Lung-ch'üan type of dragon kiln. In other words it was inclined and
may have had more than one chamber. Kiln furniture included large five-
spurred disc-type stands, and saggars.

Nearly all the material found was wheel-made. The bowls, with flared or
everted rim, occasionally straight rimmed, had flat bases; it was exceptional to
find a ring foot. The bowls had slightly raised ribs on the outside. There were
also many small models of birds and animals.

The body colour was generally grey, but in some cases tended to be yellowish. About eight per cent of the material had a light-yellow glaze, other colours being green and brown; the rarest and most attractive colour was a rather bright yellow. Most vessels were thickly glazed, the surface glassy and usually crazed.

Mo-ma Shan site was a small one producing a ware similar to that of Ch'ing-yang-kung using a brown earthenware body.[12] The bowls were small with well-rounded walls constricted below a slightly everted rim. The drawings published indicate that the bases were flat or slightly concave. The jars seem to have been the usual robust T'ang type with lugs at the base of the short wide neck.

This short summary of the meagre information available is tantalizing, and it is to be hoped that more will be published soon. Particularly interesting is the use of green and brown underglaze painting at Ch'ing-yang-kung.

12. *WW* 1966, No. 2, pp. 60–1.

Chapter 6

YÜEH WARES

The distinctive grey stoneware covered with a thin olive-green glaze, which has long been called Yüeh, was one of the most valuable commodities of the province of Chekiang. It was much sought after in China and exported throughout Asia and even to Egypt. First found overseas in 1910 at Samarra, the Abbasid capital not far from Baghdad, it was at first simply identified as a Chinese ware.[1] Not until James Marshall Plumer visited the kiln sites in northern Chekiang in 1936,[2] sites originally discovered by Nakao in 1930, did it become certain that the fragments found by Sarre in 1910 and 1913 at Samarra originated in the region of the Shang-lin Lake in northern Chekiang.

The great quantities of Yüeh found abroad have primarily served to prove commercial contacts, as in the case of Fostat, but only to a limited extent have they helped confirm dating of archaeological sites as for instance Samarra.

Not much is known about Yüeh ware in the T'ang dynasty, and virtually nothing at all between the last few years of the sixth century and the year 810, when we encounter the earliest dated T'ang piece, a ewer, a product of northern Chekiang of the Shang-lin Hu type (Plate 94).[3] The ewer is characterized by the ebullient contours that are such a marked feature of the T'ang tradition. Excavated in 1936, it is now in the Peking Palace Museum. This brings us to the whole question of what is meant by Yüeh.

The princedom of Yüeh was in the territory of modern Chekiang and Kiangsu, territory approximately the same as that of the ancient kingdom of Wu-Yüeh. This kingdom had existed in the Warring States period (c. 481–221 B.C.) and again in the Three Kingdoms (A.D. 219–316) following the fall of Han. The later Yüeh of late T'ang times was established by Ch'ien Liao in A.D. 893 when the decline of the T'ang dynasty was already far advanced. At one time the name Yüeh used to be applied with little discrimination to a wide range of stonewares characterized by a grey body and bluish, greenish or yellowish-

1. F. Sarre, *Die Ausgrabungen von Samarra, Band II, Die Keramik von Samarra*, Berlin, 1925, Tafel XXV, figs. 4 and 6.
2. J. M. Plumer, 'Certain celadon potsherds from Samarra traced to their source', *Ars Islamica*, IV, 1937, p. 195.
3. Illustrated in colour in *STZ* 1976, Vol. 11, p. 106, pl. 83.

olive glaze from many parts of China. However, following the publication of Gompertz' *Chinese Celadon Wares* in 1958, the practice was gradually adopted of applying the name only to the wares of whatever date originating in northern Chekiang, where many tombs and kiln sites have now been excavated or archaeologically surveyed. More recently still, largely as the result of archaeological work, it has become customary to reserve the name for those wares produced only from the T'ang dynasty onward, and indeed the Chinese tend to apply it only to the finest quality wares of the ninth and tenth centuries. In reserving the name Yüeh in this way the justification is to be found in the literature of the period, for with the exception of the *Ch'a-ching* of the eighth century it was not until the late eighteenth century that reference is found in the texts to Yüeh-yao. The Chinese themselves now refer to all the earlier products of the region, as well as less fine quality ones of T'ang and later, as greenwares.[4]

The characteristics which distinguish the stonewares of northern Chekiang had, of course, already been established long before the beginning of T'ang. The body is dense, fine grained and of a variable but fairly light grey colour covered with a glaze which is generally transparent. It varies from a bluish tone through green to yellowish according to the degree of reduction or oxidation, or more usually overfiring.

In the T'ang period itself, the troublesome gap between the latter part of the sixth century and the first half of the ninth century has yet to be filled. It is a surprisingly long period for which very little real evidence of ceramic production is at present available. The reason can only be that the sites most likely to produce the needed evidence of continuity have still to be located. In time no doubt this will be done and the chronological succession satisfactorily demonstrated.

The most prolific and important group of kilns working in the latter part of the T'ang period was around the great lake of Shang-lin, in Yü-yao Hsien, from which most of the specimens of top quality have probably come, but there are other groups of kilns which also deserve attention. The excavations at Yin Hsien not far from Ning-po on the coast, others south-west of Shang-lin Hu at Shang-yü, and farther south still at Chin-hua will certainly need careful study in the future, while Wên-chou, the important port south of Ning-po, seems at one time to have been well known for the high quality of its greenwares,[5] but here the body seems to have been whitish. At almost all the sites known a striking feature of the northern Chekiang kilns is the unity of style, whatever the quality may be. Similar shapes, similar decorative techniques and designs are found, the distinctions between one kiln's product and that of another

4. The Japanese employ the term 'old Yüeh' for the pre-T'ang products of northern Chekiang, also *seiji* as a general term for green-glazed wares. But see also W. Watson, 'Chinese ceramics from Neolithic to T'ang', *TOCS*, 38, 1969–71, pp. 13–32, especially pp. 23–4.
5. *KK* 1962, No. 10, p. 531 et seq. The Hsi-shan kiln south-west of the city apparently produced the best material.

94 Yüeh ware EWER. Ht. 13.4 cm (5.3 in)
From the tomb of a Lady Wang Shu-wen at Shao-hsing, dated to
A.D. 810

being virtually impossible to define as most kilns seem to have produced more
than one quality of ware. There may turn out to be refinements in the
treatment of the individual decorative motifs, however, and these may in turn
help to distinguish different groups of kilns.

The finest Yüeh, now by common consent, came from the Shang-lin Hu
kilns, some of which came into operation as early as the fifth century although
the finest quality wares to which we can attribute a T'ang date only seem to
have appeared in the late eighth or early ninth century. On the evidence of
excavations in northern Chekiang, it appears that during the seventh and

eighth centuries there was a gradual drift eastwards of the more important centres of manufacture.[6] A key piece in this shift eastwards, particularly to Shang-lin Hu is the ewer mentioned above, dated to A.D. 810 (Plate 94). This is supplemented by a vase with an exaggerated flaring neck and dished mouth-rim, dated A.D. 850, from a site to the east of the lake.[7] On the basis of the decorative technique and the motifs employed it is now becoming possible to date a large group of olive-green or yellowish-glazed stonewares of high quality to the late ninth century. There is however no very clear distinction between late ninth- and tenth-century material, and the Chinese in recent literature treat the two centuries together in their consideration of Chekiang wares. In the absence of dated material from either tombs or kiln sites, it might seem best to adopt a similar stance, except with regard to a small number of late tenth-century examples which will be mentioned later.

As far as it is possible to trace the development of Yüeh, the pattern is one in which, on the vertical forms, the contours gradually become more severe with a clearer demarcation being introduced between the neck and shoulder than is the case with the Peking ewer.

Ewers seem to have been particularly popular, or it may perhaps appear so because of their distinctive character, and the fact that they are more easily identified than bowls or dishes. The body gradually became more ovoid, and often lobed, or in some manner divided into vertical sections, but generally with firm horizontal lines defining the junction at the base of the neck and also quite often at the edge of the contracting shoulder (Plates 96 and 97). The neck became longer, but still flared at the lip. The spouts, which the potters do not seem to have been very good at, are much longer than those of earlier times, and tend to bend outwards in rather an awkward curve (Plate 97). The handles are of simple strap type, occasionally ribbed.

The bodies were sometimes incised and carved with floral decorations. On quite a number of such decorated pieces the designs ran over from one vertically defined panel to another, cutting across the formal structure and breaking the rhythm of the rising line (Plate 96). In other examples the true verticality was reinforced by carved decorations of rising petals, which seem to uphold the body. In one such case (Plate 98) the contour may be changed by cutting off the rising line and making the shoulder a straight sloping one. It will be noticed that on the shoulder of this piece there are small press-moulded reliefs applied to the shoulder, and this sometimes occurs also on other shapes.

In the course of the tenth century this pattern of tall ovoid body and long neck persisted, and is also found on vases. In later examples, running well into the tenth century, the mouth of the vase was often cupped, while at the junction of neck and shoulder small loops were added, and in some cases a band of rather emphatic pastry-work was applied to the shoulder (Plate 99). These

6. M. Tregear, *Catalogue of Chinese Greenwares in the Ashmolean Museum*, Oxford, 1976, pp. 6–10.
7. *KKHP* 1959, No. 3, pp. 107–20, see pl. 2. Translated in Oriental Ceramic Society, *Chinese Translations*, No. 6.

95 Yüeh ware EWER. Glazed
all over and fired on spurs
on the foot-ring.
Ht. 21.23 cm (8.3 in)
Late 9th century
Ashmolean Museum

96 (*below left*) EWER with
carved floral decoration
overlapping the panels of the
body. Foot-ring ground
down. Ht. 15.5 cm (6.1 in)
9th–10th century
Ashmolean Museum

97 (*below right*) EWER with
reliefs on shoulder and
weakly curved long spout.
Fired on spurs on the foot-
ring. Ht. 17.47 cm (6.9 in)
9th–10th century
Ashmolean Museum

98 EWER with carved petals and straight, almost horizontal shoulder. Fired on
    white spurs on the base. Ht. 19 cm (7.5 in)
    Shang-lin Hu, 10th century
    Ashmolean Museum

vases with cupped mouth have generally had lids, and occasionally these were
made to resemble inverted lotus-leaves (Plate 100). The foot was made with a
slight spread, and was either straight cut on the inside, or sloping to the base,
which was either glazed or unglazed, although the latter seems to have become
more common as time passed. Some of these have been identified with the
Shang-lin Hu kilns, but others with a very pale body and exceptionally pale
green glaze have not so far been satisfactorily traced to a specific kiln.[8]

8. Tregear identifies two examples in the Ashmolean as being of Shang-lin Hu type. See nos. 187
and 190. Others with a whitish body may come from farther south towards Wên-chou and
Li-shui.

99 Yüeh VASE with carved decoration, incised details and an applied pastry-work band on the shoulder. Ht. 38 cm (14.9 in) 10th century
Museum of Fine Arts, Boston

100 Yüeh VASE with cupped mouth and leaf-shaped lid.
     Carved and incised decoration overlapping the body
     panels. Glazed base, and a ring of spur-marks within the
     foot-ring. Ht. 41.9 cm (16.5 in)
     10th century
     Ashmolean Museum

101 EWER with incised
    decoration under a
    very thin evenly-
    applied glaze.
    Ht. 14.6 cm (5.7 in)
    10th century
    *Metropolitan
    Museum, New York*

102 Another view
showing the dragon
emerging from waves

There are of course exceptions to this apparent preference for tall ovoid shapes, as for instance in the rather unusual tenth-century spherical ewer in the Metropolitan Museum in New York, which has very fine incised decoration organized in medallions (Plates 101 and 102). It has a straight foot-ring and a glazed base which carries the elongated white fire-clay scars of the firing-stand arranged in the rough circle so characteristic of the best of the Shang-lin Hu type material.

Although the Chinese reports indicate that bowls and dishes occur most frequently on the sites so far investigated, relatively few can be confidently assigned to the T'ang period itself. They vary a great deal in quality, from a thick body with a yellowish-olive glaze to a thin body with a greenish or even silvery glaze of the type to which name *pi-sê-yao*, 'reserved colour ware', is attached.

Some pieces are unusual in having what superficially appears to be an underfired glaze, which in fact is not underfired, but apparently a deliberate effect. The glaze is comparatively thick, opaque and generally greenish grey with a curious waxy surface. Bowls are of a number of different kinds, one of which is straight flaring sided and rather low; the second has slightly rounded sides and is usually four-lobed, and a third type is what the Chinese describe as flower-shaped, often on a high spreading foot with rounded sides spreading slightly to an everted lip; usually there are four or five lobes.

The first type of bowl (Plates 103 and 104), generally has a low wide foot-ring with a small central recess. Some are glazed all over and then have the foot and base roughly wiped clean while others are entirely unglazed on the foot and the base. Both were fired on five or six fire-clay supports, which on the glazed ones leave unsightly whitish scars, and on the unglazed ones leave reddish haloes. It was not uncommon to stack these with small buttons of fire-clay between each bowl so that only the one on the top of the stack was unscarred inside. A large proportion of this type has a yellowish or even a brownish-green glaze, and this colour appears to be deliberately achieved.

The second type, with rounded sides four-lobed at the rim, has a square-cut foot-ring which is quite thin. This type varies a great deal in quality. Some are fired on the foot-ring, which may be glazed, the firing-stand leaving small whitish scars, or if unglazed, reddish haloes. Like the first type they are often yellowish or brownish green in colour.

The third type, the so-called flower-shaped bowls (Colour Plate O), and a bracket-lobed series (Plate 105), are among the most elegant and are usually of the very finest quality. These are glazed all over and are almost always a fine olive-green. In the firing they are supported on the base by the elongated type of fire-clay pads arranged in an untidy circle.

The decoration is limited to fine incising until into the tenth century when some specimens are found with carved and incised designs, some of them with combed details. The floral designs seem to have been preferred and there are a few examples with lotus-petals carved round the outside. The majority have

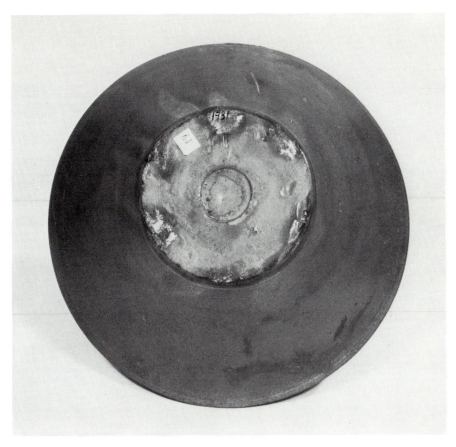

103 Conical Yüeh BOWL with small recess in the centre of the roughly glazed base,
     scarred by the six clay supports on which it was fired. Diameter 15 cm (5.9 in),
     of base 6.9 cm (2.7 in)
     Late 9th century
     Percival David Foundation Study Collection

104 Profile view of the conical Yüeh BOWL (Plate 103)

105 Bracket-lobed DISH fired on elongated white fire-clay spurs ordered roughly in
a circle. Diameter 15.7 cm (6.2 in)
Late 10th century
Fitzwilliam Museum, Cambridge

rather sketchy decoration but there are some high-quality examples in which
there are both ribbons and simple designs of birds.

It would seem that the best of the second type and all the third, together with
the finest examples of other shapes, belong to the class known as *pi-sê-yao*,
'reserved colour ware'. This class is traditionally believed to have been made at
officially established and supervised kilns in the vicinity of Shang-lin Hu and
reserved for the use of the princes of Wu-Yüeh. The local history states that
official kilns were established there in the T'ang to Sung period, and Wang
Shih-lung believes that they were set up and that *pi-sê-yao* began to be made at
some time early in the tenth century.[9] Unfortunately there are great numbers
of kilns scattered around Shang-lin Hu and at present we have no means of

9. *WW* 1958, No. 8, p. 42 et seq.

N Hard white earthenware DISH with moulded decoration. No foot,
and fired on three small spurs. Width 14.3cm (5.6in)
9th century, perhaps from Hunan
Private collection. See page 96

O Yüeh flower-shaped BOWL. Ht. 7.4cm (2.9in), Diameter 11.1cm
(4.4in)
10th century
Victoria and Albert Museum. See page 110

P Yüeh BOX with incised decoration; slightly concave base. Diameter 12.3cm (4.8in)
10th century
Percival David Foundation. See page 116

distinguishing official kilns from private kilns, although Huang-shan Shan at
the south-east corner of the lake seems one likely candidate.

The dishes are shallow, with a wide base and only slightly curving walls
which may be everted at the straight or lobed rim. Like the first two types of
bowl, the glaze is sometimes wiped from the foot and the pieces then fired on
small pads in the same way; indeed this seems to have been a common practice
in the latter part of T'ang and in the beginning of the tenth century, only
gradually giving way to the method of using sandy-white supports arranged in
a rough circle.

The decoration of the dishes in the earlier examples of the ninth century is
executed using a pointed tool sometimes fine, sometimes thick, and incising
symmetrically organized lotus-leaf patterns (Plate 106). Some of the designs
are so fine and cursive that they have been awarded the descriptive name of 'cat
scratch' by the Japanese, a style of decoration that is also found on the
innumerable boxes (Plate 107).

Boxes form an important series and their development into the tenth century

106 DISH with lightly carved and finely incised lotus-leaf decoration. Fired
    on six spurs on the neatly cut foot-ring. Diameter 13.9 cm (5.5 in)
    9th century
    Ashmolean Museum

107 Yüeh BOX with lightly and cursively cut decoration. Very pale-grey body and thin yellowish glaze. On the neatly cut unglazed foot-ring and the unglazed edges of top and bottom half are reddish-brown scorch-marks from the supports. Diameter 7.5 cm (2.9 in)
9th century
Percival David Foundation

is more easily traced than is that of bowls and dishes. The earliest ones are round with a domed lid (Plate 107). The later boxes include many that have a much flatter top and the lid has been pressed out in a decorated mould. An exceptional example is the one with a carved lid in the Fitzwilliam Museum (Plate 109). Most have a flat or slightly concave base, but some have a neat square-cut foot-ring. If there is a foot-ring that is splayed and the piece has been fired on the base instead of on the ring, it is likely to be later, well into the tenth century. The two sections of the boxes were fired at the same time, the parts being separated to avoid sticking by placing small pads of fire-clay at

108 (*opposite above*) Yüeh BOX with carved and incised decoration. Diameter 13.3 cm (5.2 in)
10th century
Formerly Mrs. Alfred Clark Collection

109 (*opposite below*) Yüeh BOX with deeply carved lid; very pale greenish glaze on a pale body. Diameter 6.6 cm (2.6 in)
Fitzwilliam Museum, Cambridge

regular intervals around the unglazed edges of the upper and lower parts, and these frequently leave red haloes.

The decoration of Yüeh, not only of boxes, began with the simple 'cat scratch' designs which are ultimately floral in origin. The incising gradually became more precise and deliberate, and some fine examples of the early tenth century are known (Colour Plate P). Ribbon designs and decorations using birds and flowers, sometimes with scrolling filling, and also with borders similarly filled, which closely resemble those on silverware, are common.[10] Carving was also used in the tenth century, often combined with combed detail though combing does not occur on the finest quality pieces. In the late ninth or early tenth century the practice of using decorated moulds seems to have been introduced, but these were mainly for boxes, and to such decoration there is sometimes added detail using a fine point or a combing instrument. Scrolling floral decorations, pairs of birds, especially parrots, confronted butterflies, and writhing dragons are among the most popular designs and they are used whether a piece is moulded like the lid of a box, or whether it is some other vessel such as a bowl or dish.

10. A good example following silver is no. 262 in the David Foundation.

110 Yüeh WATER-POT
with small foot,
fired on spurs
leaving red haloes.
Yellowish-green
glaze. Diameter
9.3 cm (3.6 in)
7th–8th century
Ashmolean Museum

111 Yüeh WATER-POT
on four simple feet; blue-
green glaze thin and even.
Ht. 5 cm (1.9 in)
Second half of
T'ang dynasty
Ashmolean Museum

112 a & b Yüeh ware CUP-STAND with finely incised decoration. The base glazed
and the piece fired on six supports on the neatly cut foot-ring; yellowish glaze
evenly applied. A waster from Shang-lin Hu. Diameter 14 cm (5.5 in)
9th century
Percival David Foundation

113 Yüeh CUP-STAND with lobed rim and 'lotus stand' centre. Finely incised
decoration; fired on a whitish ring on the base. Diameter 13 cm (5.1 in)
Late 10th century
Ashmolean Museum

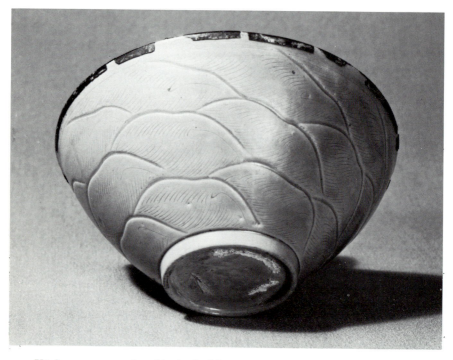

114 Yüeh BOWL carved and incised with waves, and fitted with a base gold band
at the rim. Note the white marks on the glazed base left by the firing-stand.
Diameter 14 cm (5.5 in)
Late 10th century
Percival David Foundation

One group of vessels should be noticed since it is unlike most others produced in China at this time. This is a series of small globular, or depressed globular water-pots. The earliest of this type has been attributed to the seventh or early eighth century in the catalogue of *Chinese Greenwares in the Ashmolean Museum*, where it is suggested that they came from Shao-hsing or Shang-lin Hu.[11] The curvature of the squat five-lobed body in the early examples (Plate 110) is fuller and more rounded than in the later ones. The base is concave and lacks a foot-ring. The later type has a more depressed contour, and is either raised on a low foot-ring or on four stumpy feet. A few of them are four-lobed or have raised ribs running down and widening towards each of the four feet (Plate 111). These water-pots are rarely decorated and are characterized on the whole by very high quality. They would not after all have been found among ordinary everyday household wares like the bowls and dishes, since they presuppose an owner who is literate and perhaps therefore of some social and financial standing.

Among other shapes produced at the widely distributed kilns in northern Chekiang cup-stands of several designs are found, also spittoons, and jars made in the shape of lotus-buds with high flaring feet. Some of the cup-stands have the so called 'cat scratch' decoration (Plates 112a and b), others rather fine incising and occasionally, as on the Ashmolean piece,[12] these show carved lotus-bands, although this appears a rather late example (Plate 113).

It has to be admitted that with regard to Yüeh the evidence is so inadequate that no clear conclusions can be reached at the present time. The best we can do is to indicate that the use of decoration tended to increase and become more refined as the tenth century wore on and that the finest of the tenth-century material, mainly bowls with gold and silver mounts (Colour Plate Q, Plate 114), were probably those sent to the Sung court between 960 and 990, after the princes of Wu-Yüeh had made their submission to the first Sung emperor. The kilns seem then to have begun a long slow decline. Future excavations will no doubt reveal much new information to fill the gap between the early and the late period in the T'ang dynasty and clarify the picture of the development in the ninth and tenth centuries.

11. Tregear, op. cit., nos. 130 and 131.
12. Ibid., No. 142.

Chapter 7
LIAO WARES

The Khitan tribes of Manchuria, already known to the Chinese in the early sixth century, became powerful in the late T'ang under Yeh-lü A-pao-chi, chief of the I-la tribe, and were first wholly united in A.D. 907.[1] From that time on, Khitan territory was steadily enlarged, and by 921 they had become a serious threat to the Chinese. In 923 they plundered Ting-chou and attacked Chü-yang. They continued to be a thorn in the side of the Later T'ang dynasty (923–36), for whom disaster finally came when the general Shih Ching-t'ang, who had pretensions to the throne, allied himself to the Khitans. With the help of the Khitans, Shih succeeded in ousting Later T'ang and establishing himself as the first emperor of the Later Chin in 936, but at considerable cost. He had to hand over to the Khitans sixteen prefectures in the north of Hopei and Shansi, prefectures which included Peking and Ta-t'ung. Two years later the Khitans gave stronger expression to their presence by establishing Peking as their Southern Capital, and exacting annual tribute from Later Chin of 300,000 rolls of silk, to which exactions of silver were later added.

Shih Ching-t'ang was clearly dominated by his increasingly powerful and threatening northern neighbour, accepting both demands and insults without complaint until his death in 942. His son, who succeeded him as the emperor Ch'u, disgusted with the humiliating position into which Later Chin had been pushed, decided to take a strong line against the Khitans and wrote a very stiff letter to T'ai-tsung of the Khitans, but with disastrous results. The Khitans, enraged by what they regarded as an impertinence, immediately marched south to Peking with a large army and in 944 attacked the Chin in great force inflicting a heavy defeat. Large numbers of prisoners were taken and sent back to Khitan territory in the north-east. The attack on the south continued with almost the whole of Hopei, with its major kiln sites of Ting and Tz'ŭ-chou, falling to them in 945. Chin sued for peace and a truce was agreed, but it did not last and in the following year the Khitans pushed on to Chêng-chou and K'ai-fêng, forcing the Chin into submission.

---

1. In the following paragraphs I have drawn heavily on *Liao-shih*, 'History of Liao', and on K. A. Wittfogel and C. S. Fêng, *History of Chinese Society: Liao 907–1125*, New York, 1949.

By this time the Khitans had over-extended their lines of communication, and in any case were still not sufficiently well organized administratively to maintain their hold on the conquered territory or to cope with emergencies. When rebellions broke out they were unable to suppress them without local Chinese help. Then in 947 the emperor died, and his successor withdrew to the earlier lines, at the same time adopting the Chinese dynastic name of Liao. The date 947 marks the beginning of the consolidation of the Liao empire, which now stretched from north Korea westward through Mongolia almost to Beshbalik in Central Asia. Nevertheless the threat to north China remained and the Liao inflicted a severe defeat on the Sung in 979, taking great numbers of prisoners and supplies following a Sung attempt to dislodge them from Peking.

For the next twenty years or so there was uneasy peace punctuated by skirmishes, raids and bickering. In 1003 hostilities were briefly resumed, but a lasting peace treaty was signed in the following year, under which the Chinese were forced to pay the Liao 100,000 ounces of silver and 200,000 rolls of silk a year. The Liao, remaining true to the terms of the treaty, made no further attempt at conquest. Finally they were attacked by the Jurchen from the north-east and extinguished in Manchuria in 1126.

The Liao dynasty was distinguished in the military sphere by great mobility that made rapid conquests of territory possible, and the capture of Chinese personnel relatively simple. Many skills were gained in this way, among the most important of which were agricultural skills, pottery and metalworking. Chinese influence on these three was strong, and because the civil administration of the Chinese populated areas was largely left to the Chinese themselves, those settled in Liao territory seem to have been content with their lot.

The transfer of potters from the Ting and Tz'ŭ-chou kilns naturally made a great impact on the Liao production of porcelains and stonewares, and some of the best no doubt date from after the great attack of 945, when these major kilns fell into Liao hands. The Shang-ching kiln for instance inherited influences from Ting, as did also the Kang-wa-yao-t'un kiln near Ch'ih-fêng, while some of the kilns in Liao-yang were influenced by Tz'ŭ-chou.

Both tomb and kiln finds make it clear that in the pottery there are basically two traditions in form and type. One is common to the whole northern area of China, Manchuria and Korea. The other tradition is distinctively different and is to be seen as unique to Khitan culture. The first includes all the simple bowl and vase shapes, while the second is made up of bag-shaped flasks described as cockscomb flasks, long-necked vases incorporating a phoenix head at the cupped mouth, and eccentric moulded dishes, which reflect a metalworking parentage.

White porcelain and related wares

The white porcelains associated with Liao fall into two groups. One is of early Ting type with a characteristic pure-white body and clear, sometimes ivory-toned glaze, and the other is a very fine thin ware, with a thin cold glaze which tends to have a faint bluish tinge, not unlike some of the early *ch'ing-pai*, for which it can sometimes be mistaken. The body of this second type often has tiny black or brownish specks, but this does not appear to affect the translucency of the thinner-glazed pieces.

115   White, lobed porcelain BOWL. *Kuan* inscribed on base.
Diameter 13.5 cm (5.3 in)
Early 10th century
C. Kempe Collection

Most of the best examples of both types are simple bowls with conical or slightly rounded sides and a straight rim, or a lobed or foliated one. The lobed and foliated bowls are generally rather shallow and the foot-ring low, thin and square cut (Plate 115); the Ting type examples are usually thicker in the foot-ring (Plate 116).

Some of the most distinguished bowls are marked on the glazed base with the characters *kuan*, 'official', or *hsin-kuan*, 'new official'. There are a few white stoneware jars and vases with the same characters cut into the unglazed base. Most of these marked pieces have come from Liao tombs of the tenth century. There do not appear to be any at present that can certainly be dated later than this, although it is probable that the small hemispherical jar in Tokyo National Museum, which is a Ting piece, is later. It does not seem possible to make any very clear distinction between *kuan* and *hsin-kuan* examples, beyond saying that they were likely to have been made at different kilns. Both marks appear on both the Ting and the true Liao-made wares, the latter including a wider range of shapes than is the case with Ting.

The earliest of the *kuan*-marked pieces so far recorded are those from the princely tomb at Ta-ying-tzŭ in Ch'ih-fêng dated A.D. 959.[2] Here there were two conical bowls and two multilobed bowls, the rims of the latter being bound in gilt metal. The white porcelains and stonewares in this tomb were particularly numerous and varied. There were cockscomb flasks, tall vases with long thin necks and dished mouths (Plate 117), some small round jars, and a

116 White bracket-lobed BOWL. Diameter 18.2 cm (7.2 in)
     10th century
     Freer Gallery of Art

ewer with an almost spherical body, very similar to that in the Fitzwilliam Museum (Plate 118). The *kuan*-marked pieces are described as being early Ting, but the jars and ewer are identified as Liao material of good craftsmanship imitating Ting.

A later development, probably of the early eleventh century, was the use of moulds for making bowls and dishes in which low-relief decoration was incorporated. Most examples are square with somewhat irregular sides and rims (Plate 119), but there was also a delight taken in eccentric forms such as the butterfly dish (Plate 120). The more richly decorated examples are often quite elaborate in the organization of designs that are well thought out to suit

2. 'Chih-fêng Hsien Ta-ting-tzŭ Liao mu fa-chüeh pao-kao', *KKHP*, No. 13, 1956, pp. 1–26, Tomb I.

117　White VASE with dished mouth. Inscribed on base *kuan*.
Ht. 40.3 cm (15.8 in)
From Chih-feng

118 White porcellanous EWER. Ht. 20 cm (7.8 in)
     10th century
     Fitzwilliam Museum

the shapes.[3] Most of the moulded pieces are thicker and sturdier than the thin
kuan-marked bowls. The more characteristically Liao shapes in white wares
are generally whitish stoneware and include one form which can only be
described as a spouted vase. It has a roughly ovoid body with a tall, often
horizontally ribbed neck, and a dished mouth, the fairly short spout springing

3. There are several in the Carl Kempe Collection: see Nos. 390–3 in the catalogue.

119   Moulded white porcelain DISH. Width 11.5 cm (4.5 in)
C. Kempe Collection

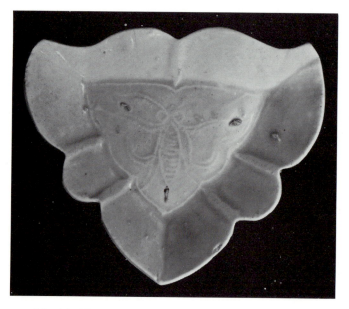

120   Moulded butterfly-shaped DISH. Width 9.3 cm (3.6 in)
C. Kempe Collection

121 Spouted VASE with cupped mouth. Ht. 27.9 cm (10.9 in)
Royal Ontario Museum

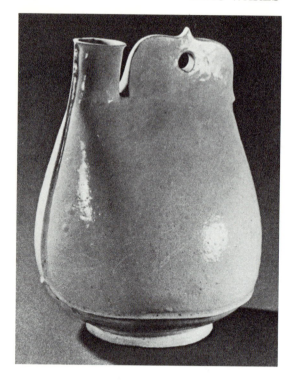

122 'Cockscomb' FLASK.
White porcellanous
ware. Ht. 23.5 cm
(9.2 in)
Chinese museum

from the rounded shoulder. Later, in the eleventh century, the dished mouth becomes cupped (Plate 121) and the body heavier and sometimes incised with petal designs. There are a few examples with coloured glazes on a buff stoneware body.

The flask shape described as a cockscomb flask is unique to the Liao culture and reflects the semi-nomadic and pastoral background of the Khitan people in the direct transfer into the ceramic medium of a leather bottle-shape.[4] It occurs in white stonewares and in the green-glazed and amber-glazed wares, those with coloured glazes first being covered with a white slip. A few white examples have green splashing or spotting down the lines where in the leather original there would have been stitching or studs.

The earliest examples had a rather round body drawn in a little and flattened towards the top where there is a bracket-shaped crest, which gives the form its name (Plate 122); in the centre of the crest is a single hole, presumably intended for suspension. The spout, which is straight tubular, is separated from the crest, often with the imitation of a cord round the base at the junction with the body. Very few of these are decorated and they occur in both high-fired and low-fired wares.

The second stage, which can be dated to about the middle of the tenth

4. In outlining the tentative chronology I have relied on Liu Wên-hsin's 'Liao-tzǔ chien-shu', *WW* 1958, No. 2, pp. 10–20. Excavations since the publication of this valuable article have tended to confirm Liu's scheme.

Q Yüeh BOWL with carved decoration of dragons rising from waves. Diameter 14.5cm (5.7in)
Second half of 10th century
Percival David Foundation. See page 119

R   Liao polychrome-glazed INK-STONE Diameter 18.3cm (7.2in)
    11th century
    Museum für Ostasiatische Kunst, Staatliche Museen Preussischer Kulturbesitz, Berlin.
    See page 136

123 FLASK with stopper.
Green glazed.
Ht. 29 cm (11.4 in)
Chinese museum

century, saw the development of a flattened body with two holes in the upstanding crest, now modified in shape so that it lacks the bracket profile (Plate 123). The base is flat and unglazed. The spout is usually short and may have a small stopper. The tall, rather flat sides were decorated either with incised scrolling or floral designs, or with applied dragon or peony reliefs; the rarest decoration is applied-relief figures, or modelled figures seated astride the crest (Plate 124).

The next stage in the development of the shape was to make it much rounder and taller still, with a notably bag-shaped profile, often with mock stitching and studs (Plate 125). The upstanding crest was converted into a finger-pinched loop handle and the spout was made slightly narrower and taller (Plate 126). The vessel now stands on a ring foot. This shape seems to appear about the turn of the century and soon became less bag-shaped and rounder all the way up, while the spout became much taller. By this time it was more truly a ceramic vase-shape, with only slight flattening at the top. These late examples were mostly monochrome glazed and were rarely decorated.

One other type was quite different. It was very squat and round, with a flat bottom, very short tube mouth, and a handle that was low and flat (Plate 127). It was reminiscent of a bag shape, the suggestion being reinforced in some cases by cordon decoration. These are very rare and always of porcellanous

124 FLASK with stopper and modelled figures. Green glazed. Ht. 31.9 cm (12.5 in)
Boston Museum of Fine Arts

125 FLASK with rope handle and mock studs. Green glaze over a white slip. Ht. 30.5 cm (12 in)
Late 10th century
National Trust, Ascott Collection

126 FLASK with pinched handle. Whitish stoneware, slipped and amber glazed. Ht. 30.5 cm (12 in)
10th–11th century
Formerly Sotheby's

material. The type is difficult to date, as although it bears a strong resemblance to the silver example of T'ang date found at Ho-chia Ts'un in Hsi-an,[5] the only example from a Liao excavation is from a tomb that cannot certainly be dated before the early or middle eleventh century. However, also in the tomb was an example of one of the second-stage type with stopper intact, so it may be that both pieces were heirlooms.

Another eccentric shape, in which the Liao potters appear to have let their creative imagination run free, is a fish-shaped water-dropper.[6] A number of

5. Illustrated in colour in *WW* 1972, No. 1, Pl. 3.
6. *WW* 1977, No. 12, Pl. 6, fig. 1 where it is described as *lung-yü*, 'dragon-fish'.

these are known and are usually of good quality. The one illustrated (Plate 128) is provided with large wing-like fins flattened against the body and resembles another one of pale celadon colour recently found in the tomb of early or middle eleventh-century date referred to above. The shape is perhaps adopted as a reference to the fish-dragon symbolic of literary aspiration, for the carp that leaps the Dragon Falls of the Yellow River is transformed into a dragon, and represents the man successful in examinations.

The excavation of kiln sites indicates that white wares of some kind were made at most groups of kilns, with good material particularly from Shang-ching at kilns just south of Lin-tung,[7] at Kang-wa-yao-t'un near Ch'ih-fêng,[8] and in the Chiang-kuan-t'un group in Liao-yang in the south-east.[9] Quite recently at Lung-ch'üan-wu near Peking a new kiln site was found, which only produced white wares, but these were not all of the highest quality.[10] It is believed to have been in operation from about A.D. 958 to 1113. The wares are broadly divided into two groups. The first is a fine quality ware with a pure white body and a glaze with a cold, slightly bluish tinge, especially where it lies thickly; it may also have tear-marks. The second is a coarse-bodied type, the pieces not being fully glazed. The glaze is white and not particularly glossy. Comparative material was found at a nearby tomb dated by inscription to A.D. 1097.[11]

At Shang-ching, the old Superior Capital, the kiln evidently operated only for a brief period of about two years, but the quality of the ware was good. Koyama, who visited the site before the last war and again in 1944, states that it was an official kiln, and that he found more than a dozen sherds among those excavated which were inscribed with the character *kuan*.[12] His conclusion conflicts with the Chinese reports, and Liu Wên-hsin, who was well acquainted with Koyama and is also very familiar with the sites, states categorically in his report that Shang-ching was not an official kiln, although a few *kuan*-marked sherds were found, but was one set up either by a wealthy aristocrat or a monastic foundation of the late eleventh century.[13] More recently, in 1975, Fêng Tung-ch'ien made it clear that no official kiln was yet known.[14] However, later in the same year a saggar was found containing a marked piece at a new site to the west of Ch'ih-fêng;[15] the report has still to be published, but this may

7. *KKHP* 1958, No. 2, pp. 97–107, a report by Liu Wên-hsin.
8. *WW* 1958, No. 2, p. 18, paragraph 4.
9. Ibid. p. 18, paragraph 5.
10. *WW* 1978, No. 5, pp. 26–32. See also *WW* 1964, No. 8, pp. 49–53. The contents of a pagoda containing an octagonal stone sutra-box inscribed and dated 1013.
11. 'Chin-nien lai Pei-ching fa-hsien ti chi-tsuo Liao-mu', *KK* 1972, No. 3, pp. 35–40, and Plates 11 and 12.
12. F. Koyama, 'Liao pottery wares', *TOCS*, 34, 1962–3, pp. 69–82; see especially p. 75.
13. See note 7 above.
14. 'Hsieh-mao-t'ai Liao-mu ch'u-t'a ti t'ao-tz'ŭ-ch'i', *WW* 1975, No. 12, pp. 40–8, especially pp. 44–45.
15. 'Liao-ning Pei-piao shui-ch'üan i-hao Liao-mu fa-chüeh chien-pao', *WW* 1977, No. 12, pp. 4–51, footnote no. 20.

127 FLASK of white
porcellanous ware.
Diameter 17 cm (6.7 in)
10th century
Chinese museum

128 Fish-shaped porcelain WATER-DROPPER. Length 19.7 cm (7.7 in)
10th century
Tokyo National Museum

129 Green-glazed VASE.
     Ht. 33 cm (13 in)
     Asian Art Museum
     of San Francisco

130 Phoenix-head VASE with incised
     floral decoration; green glazed.
     Ht. 38.2 cm (15 in)
     Tokyo National Museum

turn out to be an official kiln. It is suggested that this may be the porcelain kiln recorded in the Yüan *Ta i-t'ung chih*, the Yüan geographical record.

  Whatever answers may be found to the question of official kilns it is clear that white wares with *kuan* marks were made at a number of different places of which the Ting kilns were probably the earliest. What is interesting is that in no eleventh-century tomb has a *kuan*-marked piece so far been found, and only in a pagoda dating to A.D. 1014 have some Ting ewers and jars so marked been found, and these are almost identical with those found in the pagoda in Ting-hsien dated to A.D. 995, which also included a *kuan*-marked piece.[16]

16. Ibid., fig. 22, and 'Hopei Ting-hsien fa-hsien liang-tsuo Sung-tai t'a-chi', *WW* 1972, No. 8, pp. 39–48, and Pls. 6–7.

Coloured-glazed wares

Both earthenwares and stonewares were made which have either a green or an amber-brown glaze, and both types of ware were covered first with a white slip to conceal the coloured body. The stonewares had to be biscuit fired because, as seems most likely, the glazes were fluxed with lead and so would not withstand the high stoneware temperature. The bodies were usually buff or pinkish buff and variable in texture.

It was the practice on tall vases with long expanding necks (Plate 129), vases with phoenix heads and cupped mouth (Plates 130 and 131), and on the later cockscomb flasks to apply the slip to only about three-quarters of the body.

131 Phoenix-head VASE with amber glaze; note the white slip bottom right. Ht. 37 cm (14.5 in)
10th–11th century
Honolulu Academy of Arts

132 Brown-glazed VASE with impressed decoration. Ht. 32.6 cm (12.8 in)
10th century
Excavated at Holinkoerh in Inner Mongolia

This meant that to ensure good glaze-colour the glaze could not be applied below this line. In fact it was common to apply the glaze by dipping and leaving a wide band of slip untouched by glaze. Decoration when used was confined to simple floral motifs incised into the body before glazing. On the smaller pieces like jars and ewers, the decoration was more elaborate with applied reliefs and rouletted and impressed designs, and both slip and glaze were much more lavishly applied.

This last group is probably the earliest, as the handsome brown-glazed earthenware vase from a tomb dated to late T'ang or early Liao, i.e. late ninth or early tenth century, suggests (Plate 132).[17] This is a good example and confirms the north-eastern drift of the lead-glazing tradition. The ewers and small jars with impressed and applied relief decoration under a green or warm amber-brown glaze are fairly numerous (Plates 133 and 134), and date from the tenth century, although very few have been found in tombs. Of similar date, of buff earthenware and usually green glazed are small models of birds, generally parrots made for use as ewers. Other shapes on which coloured glazes occur are cups, cup-stands, stem-cups, leys-jars and a number of bowls with moulded decoration of flowers and leaves, and segmented-wave designs. These last are all brown glazed.

Polychrome-glazed wares

The use of coloured lead-glazes by the Liao is generally acknowledged to be the result of contact with late T'ang China in the north-eastern regions, where the tradition had a long history, and one which, as we have seen earlier, reached back in the Ta-t'ung area at least to the fifth century. Nevertheless it is of some interest that the Liao potters do not appear to have launched out into polychrome glazing until a considerable time had elapsed following the adoption of the green and brown glazes. Indeed the appearance of polychrome glazing whether on cockscomb flasks, of which there are a few, or on moulded dishes cannot be certainly dated before about 1060. The earliest piece in fact is an ink-stone from a tomb at Pa-lin in Mongolia dated to 1066.[18] This is glazed green and brown only, unlike the slightly similar one in Berlin (Colour Plate R).

The body material is buff or pinkish buff and variable in texture. It is always slipped, and where the decoration shows white, it is because a transparent colourless glaze has been used (Plate 135). The different coloured glazes often appear rather smudgy as though they had been carelessly dabbed on to different parts of the decoration.

The shapes include simple moulded circular dishes, circular flower-shaped

---

17. *Historical Relics Unearthed in New China*, Peking, 1972, No. 153. In addition to this and in similar style are the green *kundika* and the brown parrot-vessel from a tomb of A.D. 977; see *WW* 1972, No. 8, the Ting-hsien pagoda of A.D. 995.
18. *WW* 1958, No. 2, p. 13. The tomb was found in 1939.

133 Brown-glazed EWER
with impressed decoration.
Ht. 17.3 cm (6.8 in)
10th century
*Present whereabouts
not known*

134 EWER with applied
relief decoration;
green glazed.
Ht. 15.9 cm
(6.2 in)
10th century
*Asian Art Museum
of San Francisco*

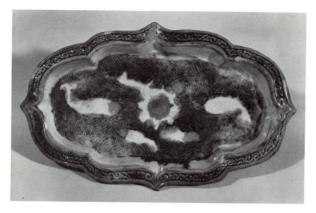

135 Moulded
earthenware DISH
with fish in a
pond; green,
amber and white
glazed. Length
27.8 cm (10.9 in)
11th century
Yamato Bunkakan

136 Moulded flower-shaped
BOWL with floral decoration
on a white ground, green,
amber and white glazed.
Diameter 14.6 cm (5.7 in)
11th century
*Asian Art Museum
of San Francisco*

137 Moulded
earthenware DISH
with flower-spray
and butterflies,
green, amber and
white glazed.
Length 29.7 cm
(11.7 in)
11th century
*Tokyo National
Museum*

dishes (Plate 136), some with an added ring foot, square dishes with straight
flaring sides irregularly shaped at the rim, and elongated quatrefoil dishes with
flat bases (Plate 137). A few other shapes such as ink-stones, or parrots and an
occasional ewer may be encountered. It was normal to fire the pieces in stacks
on spurred stands as there are always three small spur-marks on the upper
surfaces. The bases are unglazed.

Decorative schemes included peony-sprays, florets with two leaves, one on either side, or with four leaves, as a central theme for a square dish. A lotus floret placed in the centre of a dish with segmented waves all round was popular, or there may be a row of three with a water pattern on an elongated quatrefoil dish, and fish in a water pattern were also popular themes. Fine classic scrolls in low relief were particularly favoured on the narrow rim of the elongated dishes.

One small group of simple round dishes, attributed to the Liao, are straight at the rim and differ from the moulded examples in having the outlines of the decoration clearly incised into the body with the coloured glazes carefully applied to the appropriate areas (Plate 138). There is generally a wide band of plain green glaze at the rim. The decoration is mostly of ducks and other birds and flowers executed in bright yellow, green and sometimes a reddish colour, with white in a few places. Also related to these, in as much as the outlines are incised, are a small number of rather elegant bottle-vases with scrolling designs round the body in a wide band (Plate 139). These are exceptionally well made and decorated, and are characterized by a more lavish use of white. It is not known where they were made and it is not certain even from what excavations they have come. They seem to have been identified as Liao by the Japanese,

138 Earthenware DISH with incised floral decoration coloured green, amber and white with a wide band of green glaze round the rim.
Diameter 14.5 cm (5.7 in)
11th century
Formerly Sotheby Park Bernet, New York

139 Bottle VASE decorated in green, yellow and white glazes. Ht. 21.5 cm (8.5 in)
11th century
British Museum

140 Stoneware VASE with heavily incised decoration on a dark-brown ground.
Ht. 29.2 cm (11.5 in)
10th or 11th century
Victoria and Albert Museum

probably on the basis of finds in the 1930s, many of which found their way to
Japan or into the Mukden Museum. The latter was largely destroyed along
with a number of private collections in Manchuria during the war.

Tz'ŭ-chou type wares

The Liao potters were attracted by the sgraffito type of Tz'ŭ-chou wares with
which they must have become familiar in the tenth century. But in imitating

them they modified their products to such an extent that there is generally only a very slender resemblance to the Chinese examples.

The earliest examples, of vases with long slender neck and dished mouth, are strongly reminiscent of the Têng-fêng type of the tenth century.[19] In these the slip is very thin and the background is lightly cut away, but very cleanly and neatly trimmed round the edges of the floral decoration. The effect is quite striking although visually softer in impact than the more sharply and deeply cut Têng-fêng pieces. There are not very many examples of this type and it is not known at present where they were made. In the eleventh century they were replaced by a very different type, even more remote from the Chinese originals.

The new type consists of a fairly wide variety of shapes, sturdy jars, sometimes with a short neck and rolled lip, vases of *mei-p'ing* shape, always rather massive and heavy. The body is a greyish stoneware, slipped in the ordinary way and transparently glazed. The decoration is confined to a wide band often rather high up on the body of the vessel and is executed with a fine point (Plate 140). Roughly sketched floral scrolls, usually peony, with hatched details are the most common designs. The background is then painted with iron black or dark brown, sometimes neatly enough, but often carelessly so that the decoration appears messy. One kiln which seems to have produced these boldly executed, strongly made pieces has been located at Kang-wa-yao-t'un, near Ch'ih-fêng, and another has been found at Kuan-tun in Liao-yang.[20]

Also belonging to the Tz'ŭ-chou tradition are some greyish stonewares slipped in white through which decorations are heavily incised with a blunt instrument, or are rather heavily carved in an untidy manner before the application of the glaze. The range of shapes seems limited to cockscomb flasks (Plate 141), of very late tenth- to early eleventh-century date, small jars, dishes, and heavily constructed deep bowls and basins. The decorations are floral, and as is so common in Liao, a peony with a pair of leaves is the most usual design.

Black-glazed and tea-dust green-glazed stonewares

Most of these dark-glazed wares are large bottles, jars and ewers, and include the tall narrow vase with small mouth which goes by the name of 'chicken-leg vase' (Plate 142). The black-glazed wares seem to have been produced in most places where there were a number of kilns operating, but the specifically tea-dust green wares were less widely distributed.

Some of the finest black wares were made at Shang-ching. Here the body was fine-grained greyish white or almost pure white and very hard. The black glaze is dense and glassy, but occasionally has a greenish cast.[21] Not only did the Shang-ching kiln make jars and ewers, but also roof-tiles which were apparently used on the roof of the ancestral temple of T'ai-tsu of Liao at Tsu-

19. *WW* 1975, No. 12, p. 47, fig. 11.
20. *Tōki zenshū*, Vol. 14, p. 7, and *WW* 1958, No. 2, p. 18 respectively.
21. *KKHP* 1958, No. 2, p. 101.

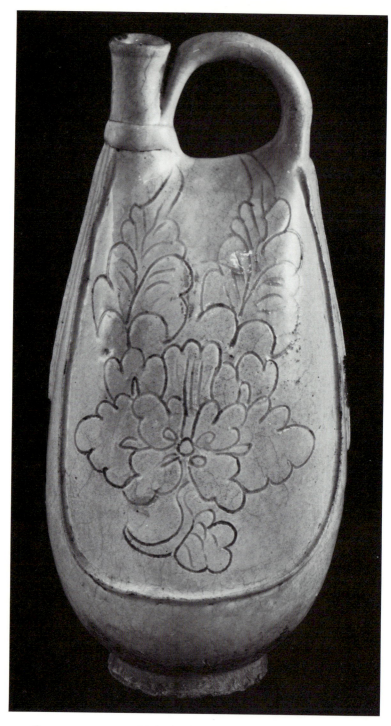

141 Stoneware FLASK with incised and carved decoration. The body
slipped in white and transparently glazed. Ht. 28 cm (11 in)
British Museum

142 Stoneware 'chicken-leg' VASE,
    dark brownish-black glazed.
    Ht. 64.8 cm (25.5 in)
    Royal Ontario Museum

143 Stoneware 'chicken-leg' VASE, very
    dark 'tea-dust' glaze. Inscribed.
    Ht. 69.5 cm (27.3 in)
    10th–11th century
    Royal Ontario Museum

chou-ch'êng. At the neighbouring kilns Pao-yin-kao-lao, barely two miles west of Shang-ching another kind of black ware was made. This had a coarse yellowish body but the glaze was again a very dense black. The firing here was carried out without saggars and the shapes included only large jars and many chicken-leg vases.

The so-called tea-dust green-glazed wares are predominantly chicken-leg vases (Plate 143) and these were also made at the Pao-yin-kao-lao kiln, with a body similar to that used for the black wares. Another important centre for the tea-dust type was Kang-wa-yao-t'un about forty miles west of Ch'ih-fêng. The body used here is coarse, yellowish and hard, while the glaze may be greyish yellow and opaque. Some examples were found at this site with inscriptions including dates round about the beginning of the eleventh century; others had Khitan inscriptions. The tea-dust glazed wares seem to have been a speciality of the district and were always fired in the same kilns. Other kilns, in all about thirty, produced a wide variety of wares.

The importance of the Liao really lies in its bridging function between the colourful earthenware tradition of T'ang and the high-fired monochrome wares, especially the white wares of Ting and the stonewares of Tz'ŭ-chou type in the Sung. There is no doubt that the Sung potters were as much inheritors of technical innovations of Liao as the Liao had been of the T'ang.

SELECT BIBLIOGRAPHY

Abbreviations used in the text:

FECB   *Far Eastern Ceramic Bulletin*
KK   *K'ao-ku*
KKHP   *K'ao-ku Hsüeh-pao*
PDF   *Percival David Foundation*
STZ   *Sekai Tōji Zenshū*
TOCS   *Transactions of the Oriental Ceramic Society*
WW   *Wên-wu*

Far Eastern Ceramic Bulletin, Michigan, 1948–60.
J. Fontein and T. Wu, *Unearthing China's Past*, Boston, 1973.
B. Gyllensvärd, *Chinese Ceramics in the Carl Kempe Collection*, Stockholm, 1964.
R. L. Hobson, *The Catalogue of the George Eumorfopoulos Collection of Chinese, Corean and Persian Pottery and Porcelain*, London, 1925–8.
K'ao-ku, 'Archaeology', Peking, from 1955.
K'ao-ku hsüeh-pao, 'Archaeological Journal', Peking.
Liao-ning Shêng Po-wu-kuan, *Liao tz'u hsüan-chi*, 'Selected Liao ceramics', Peking, 1961.
Los Angeles County Museum, *The Arts of the T'ang Dynasty*, 1957.
J. G. Mahler, *The Westerners among the Figurines of the T'ang Dynasty, China*, Rome, 1959.
New York, China Institute, *Ceramics of the Liao Dynasty*, 1973.
I. Newton, 'Chinese ceramics from Hunan', *FECB*, No. 40, 1958, pp. 3–50.
I. Newton, 'A thousand years of potting in Hunan province', *TOCS*, 26, 1950–1, pp. 27–36.
London, Oriental Ceramic Society, *Loan Exhibition of the Arts of the T'ang Dynasty*, 1955.
London, Royal Academy, *The Genius of China*, 1973.
E. H. Schafer, *The Golden Peaches of Samarkand*, Berkeley, 1963.
Sekai tōji zenshū, 'Catalogue of World Ceramics', Vol. 9, 1956 and Vol. 11, 1976. The second entirely re-written.

Tōki zenshū, Vol. 25, *Tō sansai*, 'T'ang san-ts'ai', Tokyo, 1961.

M. Tregear, *Chinese Greenwares in the Ashmolean Museum*, Oxford, 1976.

W. Watson, 'On T'ang soft glazed pottery', *Pottery and Metalwork in T'ang China* (Percival David Foundation Colloquies on Art and Archaeology in Asia No. 1), London, 1970.

W. Willetts, *Foundations of Chinese Art*, London, 1965.

Wên-wu, 'Antiquities', Peking, from 1956.

J. Wirgin, 'Some notes on Liao ceramics', *Bulletin of the Museum of Far Eastern Antiquities*, 32, Stockholm, 1960.

INDEX